SANITY IS JUST A POINT OF VIEW

"Catatonia, Doctor?" the intern asked staring down at the still figure of Luke Deveraux on the bed.

"Very strange," the doctor said. "Catatonic state at present, but it's probably only a phase. A Martian, no doubt."

"Is there any *other* reason why people go crazy, Doc?"

The doctor sighed. "There used to be other reasons. I guess they're not worth going crazy over, now. Well, that must have been when he screamed. I *would* like to know what happened, though."

"Why don't you ask me, gentlemen?"

They whirled around. Luke Deveraux was sitting up, on the edge of the bed. There was a Martian in his lap.

"Huh?" said the doctor, not very brilliantly.

Luke smiled and looked at him through eyes that were, or at least seemed, perfectly calm and sane.

He said, "I'll tell you what happened, if you're really curious. Two months ago, I went insane and I started hallucinating about Martians. I've been hallucinating ever since. Until tonight, when I snapped out of it."

"Are you—are you *sure* they were hallucinations?" the doctor asked.

"Then what," the intern asked Luke, "do you call that creature in your lap?"

Luke looked down. The Martian looked up and stuck out a long yellow tongue right into Luke's face. He pulled the tongue back with a loud slurping noise, then stuck it out again and let its tip vibrate just in front of Luke's nose.

Luke looked up and stared at the intern curiously. "There's nothing in my lap. Are you *crazy?*"

Fredric Brown

A word portion of the text is unclear here, Fredric Brown...
Bantam Books... September 1955, Copyright © 1955 by
Fredric Brown Publications, Inc.

ISBN 0-671-72120-5

First Bren printing, May 1992.

MARTIANS, GO HOME

This is a work of fiction. All the characters and events portrayed in this book are fictional, and any resemblance to real people or incidents is purely coincidental.

A Baen Book

Baen Publishing Enterprises
P.O. Box 1403
Riverdale, N.Y. 10471

ISBN: 0-671-72120-8

Cover art by Kelly Freas

First Baen printing, May 1992

Distributed by
SIMON & SCHUSTER
1230 Avenue of the Americas
New York, N.Y. 10020

Printed in the United States of America

TABLE OF CONTENTS

PROLOGUE

If the peoples of Earth were not prepared for the coming of the Martians, it was their own fault. Events of the preceding century in general and of the preceding few decades in particular should have prepared them.

One might say that preparation, in a very general sort of way, had been going on much longer than that, for ever since men had known that Earth was not the center of the Universe but only one of a number of planets circling about the same sun, men had speculated as to whether the other planets might not be, like Earth, inhabited. However, such speculation, for lack of evidence pro or con, remained a purely philosophical plane, like speculation as to how many angels could dance on the point of a pin and whether Adam had a navel.

So let's say that preparation really started with Schiaparelli and Lowell, especially Lowell.

Schiaparelli was the Italian astronomer who discov-

1

ered the *canali* on Mars, but he never claimed that they were artificial constructions. His word *canali* meant channels.

It was the American astronomer Lowell who changed the translation. It was Lowell who, after studying and drawing them, set afire first his own imagination and then the imagination of the public by claiming they were canals, definitely artificial. Proof positive that Mars was inhabited.

True, few other astronomers went along with Lowell; some denied the very existence of the markings or claimed they were only optical illusions, some explained them as natural markings, not canals at all.

But by and large the public, which always tends to accentuate the positive, eliminated the negative and sided with Lowell. Latching onto the affirmative, they demanded and got millions of words of speculation, popular-science and Sunday-supplement style, about the Martians.

Then science fiction took over the field of speculation. It took over with a resounding bang in 1895 when H. G. Wells wrote his superlative *War of the Worlds*, a classic novel describing the invasion of Earth by Martians who bridged space in projectiles fired from guns on Mars.

That book, which became tremendously popular, helped greatly in preparing Earth for invasion. And another Welles, one Orson, gave it a big assist. On Halloween eve in 1938 he put on a radio program that was a dramatization of Wells' book—and proved, although unintentionally, that many of us were even then ready to accept invasion from Mars as a reality. Thousands of people all over the country, having tuned in the program late and having missed the announcement that it was fiction, believed it as fact, believed that Martians had actually landed and were licking the hell out of us. According to their natures, some of these people ran to hide under their beds and others ran out into the street with shotguns to look for Martians.

Science fiction was burgeoning—but so was science itself, so much so that it was becoming increasingly difficult to judge, in science fictions, where the science ended and the fiction started.

V-2 rockets over the channel into England. Radar, sonar.

Then the A-bomb. People quit doubting that science could do anything it wanted to do. Atomic energy.

Experimental space rockets already pushing outside the atmosphere above White Sands, New Mexico. A space station planned to revolve around the Earth. Pretty soon the moon.

The H-bomb.

The flying saucers. Of course we know now what they were, but people didn't then and many believed firmly that they were extraterrestrial.

The atomic submarine. The discovery of metzite in 1963. Barner's theory proving Einstein's wrong, proving speeds faster than light were possible.

Anything could happen and a great many people expected it to.

Not only was the Western Hemisphere affected. People everywhere were becoming ready to believe anything. There was the Jap in Yamanashi who claimed to *be* a Martian, and got himself killed by a mob that believed him. There were the Singapore riots of 1962, and it is known that the Philippine Rebellion of the following year was sparked by a secret cult among the Moros which claimed to be in mystic communication with the Venusians and acting under their advice and guidance. And in 1964 there was the tragic case of the two American army flyers who were forced to make an emergency landing of the experimental stratojet they were flying. They landed just south of the border and were immediately and enthusiastically killed by Mexicans who, as they stepped from their plane still wearing space suits and helmets, took them to be Martians.

Yes, we should have been prepared.

But for the *form* in which they came? Yes and no. Science fiction had presented them in a thousand forms—tall blue shadows, microscopic reptiles, gigantic insects, fireballs, ambulatory flowers, what have you—but science fiction had very carefully avoided the cliché, and the cliché turned out to be the truth. They really *were* little green men.

But with a difference, and *what* a difference. Nobody could have been prepared for that.

Because many people still think that this might have a bearing on the matter, it may be well to state that the year 1964 started out in no important way different from the dozen-odd years that preceded it.

If anything, it started a trifle better. The relatively minor recession of the early sixties was over and the stock market was reaching for new highs.

The Cold War was still in the deep freeze, and the deep freeze showed no more signs of imminent explosion than at any other time since the China crisis.

Europe was more nearly united than at any time since World War II and a recovered Germany was taking its place among the great industrial nations. In the United States business was booming and there were two cars in most garages. In Asia there was less starvation than usual.

Yes, 1964 *started* well.

PART ONE

THE COMING
OF THE MARTIANS

1

TIME: Early evening of March 26, 1964, a Thursday.

PLACE: A two-room shack in desert country, near—but not too near; it was almost a mile from its nearest neighbor—Indio, California, about a hundred and fifty miles east and slightly south of Los Angeles.

On stage at rise of curtain: Luke Devereaux, alone. Why do we start with him? Why not; we've got to start somewhere. And Luke, as a science fiction writer, should have been much better prepared than most people for what was about to happen.

Meet Luke Devereaux. Thirty-seven years old, five feet ten inches tall, weighing, at this moment, a hundred and forty-four pounds. Topped with wild red hair that would never stay in place without hair dressing, and he would never use hair dressing. Under the hair, rather pale blue eyes with, quite frequently, an absent-minded stare in them; the kind of eyes that you're never sure are really seeing you even when they're looking right at you. Under the eyes, a long thin nose, reasonably well centered in a moderately long face, unshaven for forty-eight hours or more.

Dressed at the moment (8:14 P.M., Pacific Standard Time) in a white T-shirt emblazoned Y.W.C.A. in red letters, a pair of faded Levis and a pair of well-scuffed loafers.

Don't let the Y.W.C.A. on the T-shirt fool you. Luke has never been and will never be a member of that organization. The shirt belonged or had belonged to Margie, his wife or ex-wife. (Luke wasn't exactly sure which she was; she'd divorced him seven months ago but the decree would not be final for another five months.) When she had left his bed and board she must have left the T-shirt among his. He seldom wore T-shirts in Los Angeles and had not discovered it until this morning. It fitted him all right—Margie was a biggish girl—and he'd decided that, alone out here in the desert, he might as well get a day's wear out of it before considering it a rag with which to polish the car. It certainly wasn't worth taking or sending back, even had they been on more friendly terms than they were. Margie had divorced the Y.W.C.A. long before she'd divorced him and hadn't worn it since. Maybe she'd put it among his T-shirts deliberately as a joke, but he doubted that, remembering the mood she'd been in the day she'd left.

Well, he'd happened to think once during the day, if she'd left it as a joke, the joke had backfired because he'd discovered it at a time when he was alone and could actually wear it. And if by any chance she'd left it deliberately so he'd come across it, think of her and be sorry, she was fooled on that too. Shirt or no shirt, he thought of her occasionally, of course, but he wasn't sorry in the slightest degree. He was in love again, and with a girl who was the opposite of Margie in almost every way. Her name was Rosalind Hall, and she was a stenographer at the Paramount Studios. He was nuts about her. Mad about her. Crazy about her.

Which no doubt was a contributory factor to his being alone here in the shack at this moment, miles from a paved highway. The shack belonged to a friend of his, Carter Benson, who was also a writer and who occasionally, in the relatively cooler months of the year, as now, used it for the same purpose for which Luke was using it now—the pursuit of solitude in the pursuit of a story idea in the pursuit of a living.

This was the evening of Luke's third day here and he was still pursuing and still hadn't caught up with anything except the solitude. There'd been no lack of that. No telephone, no mailman, and he hadn't seen another human being, even at a distance.

But he thought that he had begun this very afternoon to sneak up on an idea. Something as yet too vague, too diaphanous, to put on paper, even as a notation; something as impalpable, perhaps, as a direction of thinking, but still *something*. That was a start, he hoped, and a big improvement over the way things had been going for him in Los Angeles.

There he'd been in the worst slump of his writing career, and had been going almost literally insane over the fact that he hadn't written a word for months. With, to make it worse, his publisher breathing down his neck via frequent airmails from New York asking for at least a *title* they could list as his next book. And how soon would he finish the book and when could they schedule it? Since they'd given him five five hundred dollar advances against it, they had the right to ask.

Finally sheer despair—and there are few despairs sheerer than that of a writer who must create and can't—had driven him to borrow the keys to Carter Benson's shack and the use of it for as long as he needed it. Luckily Benson had just signed a six months' contract with a Hollywood studio and wouldn't be using the shack for at least that long.

So here Luke Devereaux was and here he'd stay until he had plotted and started a book. He wouldn't have to finsh it here; once he'd got *going* on one he knew he could carry on with it back in his native habitat where he'd no longer have to deny himself evenings with Rosalind Hall.

And for three days now, from nine in the morning until five in the afternoon he'd paced the floor, trying to concentrate. Sober and almost going crazy at times. Evenings, because he knew that driving his brain for even longer hours would do more harm than good, he allowed himself to relax, to read and to have a few drinks. Specifically, five drinks—a quantity which he knew would relax him but would neither get him drunk nor give him a hangover the next morning. He spaced those five drinks carefully to last the evening until eleven. Eleven, on the dot, was his bedtime while here at the shack. Nothing like regularity—except that thus far it hadn't helped him much.

At 8:14 he had made his third drink—the one which would last him until nine o'clock—and had just finished taking his second short sip of it. He was trying to read but not succeeding very well because his mind, now that he was trying to concentrate on reading, wanted to think about writing instead. Minds are frequently that way.

And probably because he wasn't trying to he was getting closer to a story idea than he'd been in a long time. He was idly wondering, what if the Martians . . .

There was a knock at the door.

He stared at it for a moment in blank surprise before he put down his drink and got up out of the chair. The evening was so quiet that a car couldn't possibly have approached without his having heard it, and surely no one would have *walked* here.

The knock was repeated, louder.

Luke went to the door and opened it, looked out into the bright moonlight. At first he saw no one; then he looked downward.

"Oh, no," he said.

It was a little green man, about two and a half feet tall.

"Hi, Mack," he said. "Is this Earth?"

"Oh, *no*," Luke Devereaux said. "It *can't* be."

"Why can't it? It must be. Look." He pointed upward. "One moon, and just about the right size and distance. Earth's the only planet in the system with one moon. My planet's got two."

"Oh, God," said Luke. There is only one planet in the solar system that has *two* moons.

"Look, Mack, straighten up and fly right. Is this Earth or isn't it?"

Luke nodded dumbly.

"Okay," said the little man. "We got that settled. Now, what's wrong with *you*?"

"G-g-g," said Luke.

"You crazy? And is this the way you welcome strangers? Aren't you going to ask me in?"

Luke said, "C-come in," and stepped back.

Inside the Martian looked around and frowned. "What a lousy joint," he said "You people all live like this or are you what they call white trash? Argeth, what stinking furniture."

"I didn't pick it out," Luke said defensively. "It belongs to a friend of mine."

"Then you've got lousy taste in picking friends. You alone here?"

"That," Luke said, "is what I'm wondering. I'm not sure I believe in you. How do I know you're not an hallucination?"

The Martian hopped lightly up on a chair and sat

there with his feet dangling. "You don't know. But if you think so you got rocks in your head."

Luke opened his mouth and closed it again. Suddenly he remembered his drink and groped behind himself for it, knocked the glass over with the back of his hand instead of getting hold of it. The glass didn't break but it emptied itself across the table and onto the floor before he could right it. He swore, and then remembered that the drink hadn't been a very strong one anyway. And under the circumstances he wanted a drink that *was* a drink. He went over to the sink where the whiskey stood and poured himself half a tumbler of it straight.

He drank a slug of it that almost choked him. When he was sure that it was going to stay down he came back and sat, glass in hand, staring at his visitor.

"Getting an eyeful?" the Martian asked.

Luke didn't answer. He was getting a double eyeful and taking his time about it. His guest, he saw now, was humanoid but definitely not human. A slight suspicion that one of his friends had hired a circus midget to play a joke on him vanished.

Martian or not, his visitor wasn't human. He couldn't be a dwarf because his torso was very short proportionate to the length of his spindly arms and legs; dwarfs have long torsos and short legs. His head was relatively large and much more nearly spherical than a human head, the skull was completely bald. Nor was there any sign of a beard and Luke had a strong hunch that the creature would also be completely devoid of body hair.

The face—well, it had everything that a face should have but again things were out of proportion. The mouth was twice the size, proportionately, of a human mouth and so was the nose; the eyes were as tiny as they were bright, set quite close together. The ears were very small too, and had no lobes. In the moonlight the skin had looked olive green; here under artificial light, it looked more nearly emerald green.

The hands had six fingers apiece. That meant he probably had twelve toes too, but since he wore shoes there was no way of verifying that.

The shoes were dark green and so were the rest of his clothes—tight-fitting trousers and a loose blouse, both made of the same material—something that looked like chamois or a very soft suede. No hat.

"I'm beginning to believe you," Luke said wonderingly. He took another pull at his drink.

The Martian snorted. "Are all humans as stupid as you? And as impolite? Drinking and not offering a guest a drink?"

"Sorry," Luke said. He got up and started for the bottle and another glass.

"Not that I want one," said the Martian. "I don't drink. Disgusting habit. But you might have offered."

Luke sat down again, sighed.

"I should have," he said. "Sorry again. Now let's start over. My name's Luke Devereaux."

"A damn silly name."

"Maybe yours will sound silly to me. May I ask what it is?"

"Sure, go ahead."

Luke sighed again. "What is your name?"

"Martians don't use names. Ridiculous custom."

"But they're handy to call someone. Like—say, didn't you call me Mack?"

"Sure. We call everyone Mack—or its equivalent in whatever language we're speaking. Why bother to learn a new name for every person you speak to?"

Luke took some more of his drink. "Hmmm," he said, "maybe you've got something there, but let's skip it for something more important. How can I be sure you're really there?"

"Mack, I told you, you got rocks in your head."

"That," said Luke, "is just the point. Have I? If you're really there I'm willing to concede that you're not human and if I concede that there's no reason why I shouldn't take your word as to where you're from. But if you're not there, then I'm either drunk or hallucinating. Except that I know I'm not drunk; before I saw you I'd had only two drinks, weak ones, and I didn't feel them at all."

"Why'd you drink them then?"

"Irrelevant to what we're discussing. That leaves two possibilities—you're really there or I'm crazy."

The Martian made a rude noise. "And what makes you think those possibilities are mutually exclusive? I'm here all right. But I don't know whether or not you're crazy and I don't care."

Luke sighed. It seemed to take a lot of sighing to get along with a Martian. Or a lot of drinking. His glass was empty. He went and refilled it. Straight whiskey again but this time he put in a couple of ice cubes.

Before he sat down again, he had a thought. He put down his drink, said, "Excuse me a minute," and went outside. If the Martian was real and was really a Martian, there ought to be a spaceship somewhere around.

Or would it prove anything if there was, he wondered. If he was hallucinating the Martian why couldn't he hallucinate a spaceship as well?

But there wasn't any spaceship, hallucinated or real. The moonlight was bright and the country was flat; he could see a long way. He walked around the shack and around his car parked behind it, so he could see in all directions. No spaceship.

He went back inside, made himself comfortable and took a sizable swallow of his drink, and then pointed an accusing finger at the Martian. "No spaceship," he said.

"Of course not."

"Then how'd you get here?"

"None of your damned business, but I'll tell you. I kwimmed."

"What do you mean?"

"Like this," said the Martian. And he was gone from the chair. The word "like" had come from the chair and the word "this" came from behind Luke.

He whirled around. The Martian was sitting on the edge of the gas range.

"My God," Luke said. "Teleportation."

The Martian vanished. Luke turned back and found him in the chair again.

"Not teleportation," the Martian said. "Kwimming. You need apparatus to teleport. Kwimming's mental. Reason you can't do it is you're not smart enough."

Luke took another drink. "You got here all the way from Mars that way?"

"Sure. Just a second before I knocked on your door."

"Have you kwimmed here before? Say—" Luke pointed a finger again, "I'll bet you have, lots of you, and that accounts for superstitions about elves and—"

"Nuts," said the Martian. "You people got rocks in your heads, that's what accounts for your superstitions. I've never been here before. None of us has. We just learned the technique of long-distance kwimming. Just short-range before. To do it interplanetary, you got to savvy hokima."

Luke pointed a finger again. "Got you. How come, then, you speak English?"

The Martian's lip curled. It was a lip well adapted to curling. "I speak all your simple silly languages. All of them spoken on your radio programs anyway, and whatever other ones there are I can pick up in an hour or so apiece. Easy stuff. You'd never learn Martian in a thousand years."

"I'll be damned," Luke said. "No wonder you don't

think much of us if you get your ideas about us from our radio programs. I'll admit most of them stink."

"Then so do most of you or you wouldn't put them on the air."

Luke took a firm grip on his temper and another drink from his glass. He was beginning, finally, to believe that this really was a Martian and not a figment of his own imagination or insanity. And besides, it struck him suddenly, what did he have to lose in assuming so? If he was crazy, that was that. But if this was really a Martian, then he was missing a hell of an opportunity for a science fiction writer.

"What's Mars like?" he asked.

"None of your damn business, Mack."

Luke took another pull at his drink. He counted ten and tried to be as calm and reasonable as he could.

"Listen," he said. "I was rude at first because I was surprised. But I'm sorry and I apologize. Why can't we be friends?"

"Why should we? You're a member of an inferior race."

"Because if for no other reason it'll make this conversation more pleasant for both of us."

"Not for me, Mack. I like disliking people. I like quarreling. If you're going to go namby-pamby and pally-wally on me, I'll go find someone else to chin with."

"Wait, don't—" Luke suddenly realized that he was taking exactly the wrong tack if he wanted the Martian to stay. He said, "Get the hell out of here then, if you feel that way."

The Martian grinned. "That's better. Now we're getting somewhere."

"Why did you come to Earth?"

"That's none of your business either, but it'll be a pleasure to give you a hint. Why do people go to zoos here on your lousy planet?"

"How long do you plan to stay?"

The Martian cocked his head sidewise. "You're a hard guy to convince, Mack. I'm not *Information, Please*. What I do or why I do it is none of your business. One thing I didn't come here for is to teach kindergarten."

Luke's glass was empty again. He filled it.

He glared at the Martian. If the guy wanted to quarrel, why not? "You little green wart," he said, "damned if I don't think I ought to—"

"You ought to what? Do something to me? You and who else?"

"Me and a camera and a flash gun," Luke said, wondering why he hadn't thought of it sooner. "I'm going to get at least one picture of you. Then when I get it developed—"

He put down his glass and hurried into the bedroom. Luckily his camera was loaded and there was a bulb in the flash gun; he'd stuck them in his suitcase, not in the expectation of shooting a Martian but because Benson had told him coyotes often prowled quite close to the shack at night and he'd hoped to get a shot of one.

He hurried back, set the camera quickly, raised it in one hand and the flash gun in the other.

"Want me to pose for you?" asked the Martian. He put his thumbs in his ears and waggled his ten other fingers, crossed his eyes and stuck out a long greenish-yellow tongue.

Luke took the shot.

He put another bulb in the gun, wound the film, aimed the camera again. But the Martian wasn't there. His voice, from another corner of the room, said, "One's enough, Mack. Don't crowd your luck by boring me any worse."

Luke whirled and aimed the camera that way, but by the time he'd raised the flash gun, the Martian was gone. And a voice behind him told him not to make more of an ass of himself than he already was.

Luke gave up and put down the camera. Anyway, he had one shot on the film. When it was developed, it would either show a Martian or it wouldn't. Too bad it hadn't been color film, but you can't have everything.

He picked up his glass again. Sat down with it, because suddenly the floor was becoming just a bit unsteady. He took another drink to steady it.

"Shay," he said. "I mean, say. You catch our *radio* programs. What's the matter with television? You people behind the times?"

"What's television, Mack?"

Luke told him.

"Waves like that don't carry that far," the Martian said. "Thank Argeth. It's bad enough to listen to you people. Now that I've seen one of you and know what you look like—"

"Nuts," said Luke. "You never invented television."

"Of course not. Don't need it. If anything's going on anywhere on our world that we want to see, we just kwim there. Listen, did I just happen to find a freak, or *are* all people here hideous as you are?"

Luke almost choked over a sip he was taking from his drink. "Mean to shay—say, you think *you're* worth looking at?"

"To any other Martian, I am."

"I'll bet you drive the little girls wild," said Luke. "That is, if you're bisexual like us and there *are* Martian girls."

"We're bisexual but not, thank Argeth, like you. Do you people really carry on in the utterly disgusting way your radio characters do? Are you in what you people call love with one of your females?"

"None of your damn business," Luke told him.

"That's what *you* think," said the Martian.

And he vanished.

Luke stood up—not too steadily—and looked around to see if he had kwimmed to another part of the room. He hadn't.

Luke sat down again, shook his head to clear it, and took another drink, to fuddle it.

Thank God or Argeth, he thought, that he'd got that picture. Tomorrow morning he'd drive back to Los Angeles and get it developed. If it showed an empty chair he'd put himself in the hands of a psychiatrist, but fast. If it showed a Martian— Well, if it did, he'd decide then what he was going to do about it, if anything.

Meanwhile, getting drunk as fast as he could was the only sensible thing he could do. He was already too drunk to risk driving back tonight and the faster he drank himself to sleep the sooner he'd wake up in the morning.

He blinked his eyes and when he opened them again, there was the Martian back in the chair.

Grinning at him. "I was just in that pigsty of a bedroom, reading your correspondence. Foo, what trash."

Correspondence? He didn't have any correspondence here with him, Luke thought. And then he remembered that he did have. A little packet of three letters from Rosalind, the ones she'd written him while he was in New York three months ago, seeing his publisher and talking him out of more money on the book he was now trying to start. He'd stayed a week, mostly to renew his acquaintances among magazine editors while he was there; he'd written Rosalind every day and she'd written him three times. They were the only letters he'd ever had from her and he'd saved them carefully, had put them in his suitcase thinking to reread them here if he got too lonely.

"Argeth, what mush," said the Martian. "And what a damned silly way you people have of writing your language. Took me a full minute to break down your alphabet and correlate the sounds and letters. Imagine a language that has the same sound spelled three different ways—as in true, too and through."

"God damn it," said Luke, "you had no business reading my mail."

"Chip, chip," said the Martian. "Anything's my business that I make my business and you wouldn't tell me about your love life, Sweetie-pie, Darling, Honeybun."

"You really did read it then, you little green wart. For a dime, I'd—"

"You'd what?" asked the Martian contemptuously.

"Toss you all the way back to Mars, that's what," Luke said.

The Martian laughed raucously. "Save your breath, Mack, for making love to your Rosalind. Bet you think she meant all that hogwash she fed you in those letters. Bet you think she's as dopey about you as you are about her."

"She *is* as dopey—I mean, God damn it—"

"Don't get an ulcer, Mack. Her address was on the envelope. I'll kwim there right now and find out for you. Hold your hat."

"You stay right—"

Luke was alone again.

And his glass was empty so he made his way across to the sink and refilled it. He was already drunker than he'd been in years, but the quicker he knocked himself out the better. If possible, before the Martian came back or kwimmed back, if he really was coming or kwimming back.

Because he just couldn't *take* any more. Hallucination or reality, he couldn't help himself, he *would* throw the Martian right through the window. And maybe start an interplanetary war.

Back in the chair he started on the drink. This one should do it.

"Hey, Mack. Still sober enough to talk?"

He opened his eyes, wondering when he had closed them. The Martian was back.

"Go 'way," he said. "Get lost. Tomorrow I'll—"

"Straighten up, Mack. I got news for you, straight from Hollywood. That chick of yours is home and she's lonesome for you all right."

"Yeah? Tole you she loved me, didden I? You li'l green—"

"So lonesome for you she had someone in to console her. Tall blond guy. She called him Harry."

It partly sobered Luke for a second. Rosalind *did* have a friend named Harry, but it was platonic; they were friends because they worked in the same department at Paramount. He'd make sure and then tell off the Martian for tattling.

"Harry Sunderman?" he asked. "Slender, snappy dresser, always wears loud sport coats—?"

"Nope, this Harry wasn't that Harry, Mack. Not if he always wears loud sport coats. This Harry wasn't wearing anything but a wrist watch."

Luke Devereaux roared and got to his feet, lunged at the Martian. With both hands extended he grabbed at a green neck.

And both hands went right through it and closed on one another.

The little green man grinned up at him and stuck out his tongue. Then pulled it in again. "Want to know what they were doing, Mack? Your Rosalind and her Harry?"

Luke didn't answer. He staggered back for his drink and gulped the rest of it down.

And gulping it down was the last thing he remembered when he woke up in the morning. He was lying on the bed; he'd got that far somehow. But he was atop the covers, not under them, and fully dressed even to his shoes.

He had a God-awful headache and a hellish taste in his mouth.

He sat up and looked around fearfully.

No little green man.

Made his way to the living room door and looked around in there. Came back and looked at the stove, wondering if coffee would be worth the effort of making it.

Decided that it wouldn't since he could get some already made on his way back to town, less than a mile after he got on the main highway. And the sooner he got there and the sooner thereafter he got back to town the better. He wouldn't even clean up or pack. He could come back later and get his stuff. Or ask someone to come and get it for him if he was going to be in the looney bin for a while.

Right now all he wanted was *out* of here and to hell with everything else. He wouldn't even bathe or shave until he was home; he had an extra razor in his apartment and all of his good clothes were still there anyway.

And after that, what?

Well, after that he'd worry about what after that. He'd be nearly enough over his hang-over to think things out calmly.

Walking through the other room he saw the camera, hesitated briefly and then picked it up to take along. Might as well, before he did his heavy thinking, get that picture developed. There was still a chance in a thousand that, despite the fact that his hands had passed through it, an actual Martian and not an hallucination had been in that chair. Maybe Martians had stranger powers than being able to kwim.

Yes, if there *was* a Martian on that photograph it would change all his thinking, so he might as well eliminate the possibility before making any decisions.

If there wasn't—well, the sensible thing to do if he

could bring himself to do it would be to phone Margie and ask her the name of the psychiatrist she'd tried to get him to go to several times during their marriage. She'd been a nurse in several mental institutions before they were married and she'd gone to work in another one when she'd walked out on him. And she'd told him that she'd majored in psychology at college and, if she could have afforded the extra years of schooling, would have tried to become a psychiatrist herself.

He went out and locked the door, walked around the house to his car.

The little green man was sitting on the car's radiator.

"Hi, Mack," he said. "You look like hell, but I guess you earned the right to. Drinking is sure a disgusting habit."

Luke turned and went back to the door, let himself in again. He got the bottle and poured himself a pickup drink and drank it. Before, he'd fought off the idea of taking one. If he was still hallucinating, though, he needed one. And, once his throat had quit burning, it did make him feel better physically. Not much, but a little.

He locked the house again and went back to his car. The Martian was still there. Luke got in and started the engine.

Then he leaned his head out of the window. "Hey," he said, "how can I see the road with you sitting there?"

The Martian looked back and sneered. "What do I care whether you can see the road or not? If you have an accident it won't hurt *me*."

Luke sighed and started the car. He drove the stretch of primitive road to the highway with his head stuck out of the window. Hallucination or no, he couldn't see through the little green man so he had to see past him.

He hesitated whether or not to stop at the diner for coffee, decided that he might as well. Maybe the Martian would stay where he was. If he didn't, if he entered the diner too, well, nobody else would be able to see him anyway so what did it matter? Except that he'd have to remember not to talk to him.

The Martian jumped down when he parked the car and followed him into the diner. There weren't, as it happened, any other customers. Just a sallow-faced counterman in a dirty white apron.

Luke sat on a stool. The Martian jumped up and stood on the adjacent stool, leaned his elbows on the counter.

The counterman turned and looked, not at Luke. He groaned, "Oh, God, another one of 'em."

"Huh?" said Luke. "Another what?" He found himself gripping the edge of the counter so tightly that it hurt his fingers.

"Another Goddam Martian," said the clerk. "Can't you *see* it?"

Luke took a deep breath and let it out slowly. "You mean there are *more* of them?"

The counterman stared at Luke in utter amazement. "Mister, where *were* you last night? Out on the desert alone and without a radio or TV? Jesus, there are a *million* of them."

2

The counterman was wrong. It was estimated later that there were approximately a billion of them.

And let's leave Luke Devereaux for a while—we'll get back to him later—and take a look at things that were happening elsewhere while Luke was entertaining his visitor at the Benson shack near Indio.

As near as matters, a billion Martians. Approximately one to every three human beings—men, women and children—on Earth.

There were close to sixty million in the United States alone and an equivalent number relative to population in every other country in the world. They'd all appeared at, as near as could be determined, exactly the same moment everywhere. In the Pacific time zone, it had been at 8:14 P.M. Other time zones, other times. In New York it was three hours later, 11:14 P.M., with the theaters just letting out and the night clubs just starting to get noisy. (They got noisier after the Martians came.) In London it was 4:14 in the morning—but people woke up all right; the Martians wakened them gleefully. In Moscow it was 7:14 A.M. with people just getting ready to go to work—and the fact that many of them actually went to work speaks well for their courage. Or maybe they were more afraid of the Kremlin than of the Martians. In Tokyo it was 1:14 P.M. and in Honolulu 6:14 P.M.

A great many people died that evening. Or morning or afternoon, depending on where they were.

Casualties in the United States alone are estimated to have run as high as thirty thousand people, most of them within minutes of the moment of arrival of the Martians.

Some died of heart failure from sheer fright. Others of apoplexy. A great many died of gunshot wounds because a great many people got out guns and tried to shoot Martians. The bullets went right through the Martians without hurting them and all too frequently came to rest embedded in human flesh. A great many people died in automobile accidents. Some Martians had kwimmed themselves into moving vehicles, usually on the front seat alongside the driver. "Faster, Mack, faster," coming from what a driver thinks is an empty seat beside him is not conducive to his retaining control of the car, even if he doesn't turn to look.

Casualties among the Martians were zero, although people attacked them—sometimes on sight but more frequently after, as in the case of Luke Devereaux, they had been goaded into an attack—with guns, knives, axes, chairs, pitchforks, dishes, cleavers, saxophones, books, tables, wrenches, hammers, scythes, lamps and lawn mowers, with anything that came to hand. The Martians jeered and made insulting remarks.

Other people, of course, tried to welcome them and to make friends with them. To these people the Martians were much more insulting.

But wherever they arrived and however they were received, to say that they caused trouble and confusion is to make the understatement of the century.

3

Take, for example, the sad sequence of events at television station KVAK, Chicago. Not that what happened there was basically different from what happened at all other television stations operating with live broadcasts at the time, but we can't take *all* of them.

It was a prestige program and a spectacular, rolled into one. Richard Bretaine, the greatest Shakespearean actor in the world, was enacting a condensed-for-television version of *Romeo and Juliet*, with Helen Ferguson playing opposite him.

The production had started at ten o'clock and by fourteen minutes after the hour had reached the balcony scene of Act II. Juliet had just appeared on the balcony and Romeo below was sonorously declaiming that most famous of romantic speeches:

> *But, soft! what light through yonder window breaks?*
> *It is the east, and Juliet is the sun!*
> *Arise, fair sun, and kill the envious moon,*
> *Who is already sick and pale with grief,*
> *That thou her maid . . .*

That was just how far he got when suddenly there was a little green man perched on the balcony railing about two feet to the left of where Helen Ferguson leaned upon it.

Richard Bretaine gulped and faltered, but recovered and went on. After all, he had no evidence yet that anyone besides himself was seeing what *he* was seeing. And in any case the show must go on.

He went bravely on:

> *. . . art far more fair than she:*
> *Be not her maid, since she is envious;*
> *Her vestal livery is but sick and green—*

The word *green* stuck in his throat. He paused for breath and in that pause he heard a collective murmur that seemed to come from all over the studio.

And in that pause the little man said in a loud clear sneering voice, "Mack, that's a lot of bull, and you know it."

Juliet straightened up and turned and saw what was on the railing beside her. She screamed and slumped in a dead faint.

The little green man looked down at her calmly.

"What the hell's wrong with *you*, Toots?" he wanted to know.

The director of the play was a brave man and a man of action. Twenty years before he had been a lieutenant of marines and had led, not followed, his men in the assaults on Tarawa and Kwajalein; he had earned two medals for bravery beyond the call of duty, at a time when bravery within the call of duty was practically suicide. Since then he had put on sixty pounds and a bay window, but he was still a brave man.

He proved it by running from beside the camera onto the set to grab the intruder and carry him off.

He grabbed, but nothing happened. The little green man gave a loud raspberry, Brooklyn style. Then he jumped to his feet on the railing and, while the director's hands tried in vain to close around his ankles and not through them, he turned slightly to face the camera and raised his right hand, put thumb to nose and wiggled his fingers.

That was the moment at which the man in the control room suddenly recovered enough presence of mind to cut the show off the air and nobody who wasn't in the studio at the time knows what happened after that.

For that matter, only a fraction of the original half million or so people who had been watching the show on their television sets saw the show even up to that point, by a minute or two. They had Martians of their own to worry about, right in their own living rooms.

4

Or take the sad case of honeymooning couples—and at any given moment, including the moment in question, a lot of couples are on honeymoons, or some reasonable if less legal equivalent of honeymoons.

Take, for random example, Mr. and Mrs. William R. Gruder, ages twenty-five and twenty-two respectively, who that very day had been married in Denver. Bill Gruder was an ensign in the navy, stationed as an instructor on Treasure Island, San Francisco. His bride, Dorothy Gruder, nee Armstrong, was a want-ad taker for the Chicago *Tribune*. They had met and fallen in love while Bill had been at the Great Lakes Naval Training Station near Chicago. After Bill's transfer to San Francisco they had decided to get married on the first day of a week's leave Bill had coming, and to meet each other halfway, in Denver, for the purpose. And to spend that week in Denver as a honeymoon, after which he'd return to San Francisco and she'd go with him.

They had been married at four o'clock that afternoon and, had they known what was going to happen within a few hours, they would have gone to a hotel immediately to consummate their marriage before the Martians came. But of course they didn't know.

At that, they were lucky in one way. They didn't happen to draw a Martian immediately; they had time to prepare themselves mentally before they saw one.

At 9:14 that evening, Mountain time, they had just checked into a Denver hotel (after having had a leisurely dinner and then killing time over a few cocktails, to show themselves and each other that they had the willpower to wait until it was decently time to go to bed and that anyway they hadn't got married *just* for *that*) and the bellboy was just putting down their suitcases in the room.

As Bill was handing him a somewhat overgenerous tip, they heard the first of what turned out to be a series of noises. Someone in a room not too far away screamed, and the scream was echoed by other and more distant screams, seemingly coming from several different directions. There were angry shouts in masculine voices. Then the sound of six shots in rapid succession, as though someone was emptying a revolver. Running footsteps in the corridor.

And other running footsteps that seemed to come from the street outside, and a sudden squeal of brakes and then some more shots. And a loud voice in what seemed to be the room right next to theirs, too muffled for the words to be clear but sounding very much like swearing.

Bill frowned at the bellboy. "I thought this was a quiet hotel, a good one. It used to be."

The bellboy's face was bewildered. "It *is*, Sir. I can't imagine what in the world—"

He walked rapidly to the door and opened it, looked up and down the corridor. But whoever had been running there was out of sight around a turn.

He said over his shoulder, "I'm sorry, Sir. I don't know what's happening, but *something* is. I better get back to the desk—and I'd suggest you bolt your door right away. Good night and thank you."

He pulled the door shut behind him. Bill went over and slid the bolt, then turned to Dorothy. "It's probably nothing, honey. Let's forget it."

He took a step toward her, then stopped as there was another fusillade of shots, this time definitely from the street outside, and more running footsteps. Their room was on the third floor and one of the windows was open a few inches; the sounds were clear and definite.

"Just a minute, honey," Bill said. "Something *is* going on."

He strode to the window, threw it up the rest of the way, leaned out and looked down. Dorothy joined him there.

At first they saw nothing but a street empty save for parked cars. Then out of the doorway of an apartment building across the street a man and a child came running. Or was it a child? Even at that distance and in dim light there seemed to be something strange about him. The man stopped and kicked hard at the child, if it was a child. From where they watched it looked for all the world as though the man's foot went right *through* the child.

The man fell, a beautiful prat-fall that would have been funny under other circumstances, then got up and started running again, and the child stayed right with him. One of them was talking, but they couldn't hear the words or tell which it was, except that it didn't sound like a child's voice.

Then they were out of sight around the corner. From another direction, far off in the night, came the sound of more shooting.

But there was nothing more to see.

They pulled their heads back in, looked at one another.

"Bill," Dorothy said, "something's— Could there be a revolution starting, or—or what?"

"Hell, no, not here. But—" His eyes lighted on a quarter-in-the-slot radio on the dresser and he headed for it, fumbling loose coins out of his pocket. He found a quarter among them, dropped it in the slot and pushed the button. The girl joined him in front of it and they stood, each with an arm around the other, staring at the radio while it warmed up. When there was a humming sound from it, Bill reached with his free hand and turned the dial until there was a voice, a very loud and excited voice.

". . . Martians, definitely Martians," it was saying. "But please, people, do not panic. Don't be afraid, but don't try to attack them. It doesn't do any good anyway. Besides, they are harmless. They can't hurt you for the same reason that you can't hurt them. I repeat, they are harmless.

"I repeat, you can't hurt them. Your hand goes right through one, as through smoke. Bullets, knives, other weapons are useless for the same reason. And as far as we can see or find out, none of them has tried to hurt any human being anyway. So be calm and don't panic."

Another voice was cutting in, more or less garbling what was being said, but the announcer's voice rose in pitch to carry over the new voice. "Yes, there's one on my desk right in front of me and he's talking to me but I'm keeping my mouth so close to the mike that—"

"Bill, that's a gag, a fiction program. Like the time my parents told me about—back twenty years ago or so. Get another station."

Bill said, "Sure, honey. Sure it's a gag." He turned the dial a quarter of an inch.

Another voice. ". . . don't get excited, folks. A lot of people have killed one another or hurt themselves already trying to kill Martians, and they just don't kill. So don't try. Stay calm. Yes, they're all over the world, not just here in Denver. We've got part of the staff monitoring other stations, covering as many of them as they can, and we haven't found a station yet that's operating that isn't reporting them, even on the other side of the world.

"But they won't hurt you. I repeat, they won't hurt you. So don't get excited, stay calm. Wait, the one that's on my shoulder—he's been trying to say something to me but I don't know what because I've been talking myself. But I'm going to put the mike up to him and I'm going to ask him to reassure you. They've been being—well, impolite here to us, but I know that when he knows he's talking to millions of listeners, he'll, well— Here, fellow, will you reassure our great audience?" A different voice spoke, a voice a little higher pitched than the announcer's. "Thanks, Mack. What I've been telling *you* was to screw yourself, and now I can tell *all* these lovely people to—"

The station went dead.

Bill's arm had fallen from around Dorothy and hers from around him. They stared at one another. Then she said faintly, "Darling, try another station. That just *can't*—"

Bill Gruder reached for the dial, but his hand never got there.

Behind them in the room a voice said, "Hi, Mack. Hi, Toots."

They whirled. I don't have to tell you what they saw; you know by now. He was sitting cross-legged on the window sill they had been leaning over a few minutes before.

Neither of them said anything and a full minute went by. Nothing happened except that Bill's hand found Dorothy's and squeezed it.

The Martian grinned at them. "Cat got your tongues?"

Bill cleared his throat. "Is this the McCoy? Are you really a—a Martian?"

"Argeth, but you're stupid. After what you were just listening to, you ask that."

"Why, you damn little—"

Dorothy grabbed Bill's arm as he let go of her hand and started forward. "Bill, keep your temper. Remember what the radio said."

Bill Gruder subsided, but still glared. "All right," he said to the Martian, "what do you want?"

"Nothing, Mack. Why should I want anything *you* could give me?"

"Then scram the hell out of here. We don't want company."

"Oh, newlyweds maybe?"

Dorothy said, "We were married this afternoon." Proudly.

"Good," said the Martian. "Then I do want something. I've heard about your disgusting mating habits. Now I can watch them."

Bill Gruder tore loose from his bride's grip on his arm and strode across the room. He reached for—and right through—the Martian on the windowsill. He fell forward so hard that he himself almost went through the open window.

"Temper, temper," said the Martian. "Chip, chip."

Bill went back to Dorothy, put a protecting arm around her, stood glaring.

"I'll be damned," he said. "He just isn't *there*."

"That's what *you* think, Stupid," said the Martian.

Dorothy said, "It's like the radio said, Bill. But remember he can't hurt us either."

"He's hurting *me*, honey. Just by sitting there."

"You know what I'm waiting for," the Martian said. "If you want me to go away, go ahead. You people take your clothes off first, don't you? Well, get undressed."

Bill took a step forward again. "You little green—"

Dorothy stopped him. "Bill, let me try something." She stepped around him, looked appealingly at the Martian. "You don't understand," she said. "We—

make love only in private. We can't and won't till you
go away. *Please* go."

"Nuts, Toots. I'm staying."

And he stayed.

For three and a half hours, sitting side by side on
the edge of the bed they tried to ignore him and
outwait him. Not, of course, ever saying to one another that they were trying to outwait him, because
they knew by now that that would make him even
more stubborn in staying.

Occasionally they talked to one another, or tried to
talk, but it wasn't very intelligent conversation. Occasionally Bill would go over to the radio, turn it on,
and fiddle with it for a while, hoping that by now
someone would have found some effective way of
dealing with Martians, or would give some advice
more constructive than simply telling people to stay
calm, not to panic. Bill wasn't panicky but neither was
he in any mood to stay calm.

But one radio station was like another—they all
sounded like poorly organized madhouses—except for
those that had gone off the air completely. And nobody had discovered anything whatsoever to do about
the Martians. From time to time a bulletin would go
on the air, a statement released by the President of
the United States, the Chairman of the Atomic Energy
Commission, or some equally important public figure.
The statements all advised people to keep calm and
not get excited, that the Martians were harmless, and
that we should make friends with them if possible.
But no station reported a single incident that indicated
that anyone on Earth had succeeded in making friends
with a single Martian.

Finally Bill gave up the radio as a bad job for the
last time and went back to sit on the bed, forgot that
he was ignoring the Martian and glowered at him.

The Martian was seemingly paying no attention

whatsoever to the Gruders. He had taken a little fife-like musical instrument out of his pocket and was playing tunes to himself on it—if they were tunes. The notes were unbearably shrill and didn't form any Earthly musical pattern. Like a peanut wagon gone berserk.

Occasionally he'd put down the fife and look up at them, saying nothing, which was probably the most irritating thing he could have said.

At one o'clock in the morning, Bill Gruder's impatience exploded. He said, "To hell with this. He can't see in the dark, and if I pull down the shades before I turn off the light—"

Dorothy's voice sounded worried. "Darling, how do we *know* he can't see in the dark. Cats can, and owls."

Bill hesitated, but only a moment. "Damn it, honey, even if he can see in the dark he can't see through blankets. We can even undress under the covers."

He went over to the window and slammed it down, then pulled the shade, taking angry pleasure in reaching right through the Martian to perform both operations. He pulled down the other shade and then turned off the light. Groped his way to the bed.

And, although their feeling of a need for silence inhibited them in some ways, and they didn't feel it right even to whisper to one another, it was a wedding night after all.

They'd have been less happy about it though (and were less happy about it the next day) had they known, as everyone found out within a day or two, that not only could Martians see in the dark, but they *could* see through blankets. Or even walls. Some kind of X-ray vision or, more likely, some special ability like kwimming, enabled them to see right through solid objects. And very good vision it was too, for they could read the fine print on folded documents in closed drawers or in locked safes. They could read letters or even books without opening them.

As soon as this was learned, people knew that they could never again be *sure* of privacy as long as the Martians stayed. Even if there wasn't a Martian in the room with them, there might be one in the next room or outside the building watching them through the wall.

But that is getting ahead of ourselves, because few people learned or guessed it the first night. (Luke Devereaux, for one, should have guessed it, because his Martian had read Rosalind's letters in a closed suitcase—but then at that moment Luke didn't yet know that the Martian couldn't have simply opened the suitcase and handled the letter. And after Luke *did* have those two facts to couple together he was in no shape to do any effective coupling.) And that first night, before most people knew, the Martians must have seen plenty. Especially the thousands of them that happened to kwim into already darkened rooms and found themselves interested enough in what was going on there to keep their mouths shut for a while.

5

America's second most popular indoor sport took an even worse beating that night, and became impossible then and thereafter.

Take what happened to the gang that played poker every Thursday night at George Keller's place on the beach a few miles north of Laguna, California. George was a bachelor and retired; he lived there the year round. The others all lived in Laguna, held jobs or owned shops.

That particular Thursday evening there were six of them, counting George. Just the right number for a good game, and they *played* a good game, all of them, with the stakes just high enough to make it exciting but not high enough to hurt the losers seriously. Dealer's choice, but dealers chose only between draw poker and five-card stud, never a wild game. With all of them poker was more nearly a religion than it was a vice. Thursday nights from around eight until around one—or sometimes even two—in the morning were the highlights in their lives, the shining hours to which they looked forward throughout the duller days and evenings of the week. You couldn't call them fanatics, perhaps, but you could call them dedicated.

By a few minutes after eight they were comfortable in shirt sleeves and with neckties loosened or taken off, sitting around the big table in the living room

ready to start play as soon as George had finished
shuffling the new deck he had just broken out. They'd
all bought chips and they all had tinkling glasses or
opened beer cans in front of them. (They always
drank, but always moderately, never enough to spoil
their judgment or the game.)

George finished his shuffle and dealt the cards
around face up to see who'd catch a jack for the first
deal; it went to Gerry Dix, head teller at the Laguna
bank.

Dix dealt and won the first hand himself on three
tens. It was a small pot, though; only George had been
able to stay and draw cards with him. And George
hadn't even been able to call; he'd drawn to a pair of
nines and hadn't improved them.

Next man around, Bob Trimble, proprietor of the
local stationery store, gathered in the cards for next
deal. "Ante up, boys," he said. "This one'll be better.
Everybody gets good cards."

Across the room the radio played soft music.
George Keller liked background music and knew
which stations to get it on at any given hour of a
Thursday evening.

Trimble dealt. George picked up his hand and saw
two small pairs, sevens and treys. Openers, but a bit
weak to open on right under the gun; someone would
probably raise him. If someone else opened he could
stay and draw a card. "By me," he said.

Two more passed and then Wainright—Harry Wainright, manager of a small department store in South
Laguna—opened the pot for a red chip. Dix and Trimble both stayed, without raising, and George did the
same. The men who'd passed between George and
Wainright passed again. That left four of them in the
game and gave George an inexpensive draw to his two
small pairs; if he made a full house out of them he'd
probably have the winning hand.

Trimble picked up the deck again. "Cards, George?"

"Just a second," George said suddenly. He'd turned his head and was listening to the radio. It wasn't playing music now and, in retrospect, he realized that it hadn't been for the past minute or two. Somebody was yammering, and much too excitedly for it to be a commercial; the voice sounded actually hysterical. Besides, it was around a quarter after eight and if he had the program he thought he had, it was the *Starlight Hour*, which was interrupted only once, at the half hour, by a commercial break.

Could this possibly be an emergency announcement—a declaration of war, warning of an impending air attack, or something of the sort?

"Just a second, Bob," he said to Trimble, putting down his hand and getting up out of his chair. He went over to the radio and turned up the volume.

". . . . little green men, dozens of them, all over the studio and the station. They say they're Martians. They're being reported from all over. But don't get excited—they can't hurt you. Perfectly harmless because they're impal—im—you can't *touch* them; your hand or anything you throw at them goes right through like they weren't there, and they can't touch you for the same reason. So don't—"

There was more.

All six of them were listening now. Then Gerry Dix said, "What the hell, George? You holding up the game just to listen to a science-fiction program?"

George said, "But is it? I had the Goddam *Starlight Hour* tuned in there. Music."

"That's right," Walt Grainger said. "A minute or two ago they were playing a Strauss waltz. *Vienna Woods,* I think."

"Try a different station, George," Trimble suggested.

Just then, before George could reach out for the dial, the radio went suddenly dead.

"Damn," George said, fiddling with the dials. "A tube must have just conked out. Can't even get a hum out of it now."

Wainright said, "Maybe the Martians did it. Come on back to the game, George, before my cards get cold. They're hot enough right now to take this little hand."

George hesitated, then looked toward Walt Grainger. All five of the men had come out from Laguna in one car, Grainger's.

"Walt," George said, "you got a radio in your car?"

"No."

George said, "Damn it. And no telephone because the lousy phone company won't run poles this far out from—Oh, hell, let's forget it."

"If you're *really* worried, George," Walt said, "we can take a quick run into town. Either you and me and let the others keep playing, or all six of us can go, and be back here in less than an hour. It won't lose us too much time; we can play a little later to make up for it."

"Unless we run into a spaceshipload of Martians on the way," Gerry Dix said.

"Nuts," Wainright said, "George, what happened is your radio jumped stations somehow. It was going on the blink anyway or it wouldn't be dead now."

"I'll go along with that," Dix said. "And what the hell if there *are* Martians around; let 'em come out here if they want to see us. This is our *poker* night, Gentlemen. Let's play cards, and let the chips fall where they may."

George Keller sighed. "Okay," he said.

He walked back to the table and sat down, picked up his hand and looked at it to remind himself what it had been. Oh, yes, sevens and treys. And it was his turn to draw.

"Cards?" Trimble asked, picking up the deck again.

"One for me," George said, discarding his fifth card. But Trimble never dealt it.

Suddenly, across the table, Walt Grainger said, "Jesus Christ!" in such a tone of voice that they all froze for a second; then they stared at him and quickly turned to see what *he* was staring at.

There were two Martians. One was sitting on top of a floor lamp; the other was standing atop the radio cabinet.

George Keller, the host, was the one who recovered first, probably because he was the one of them who'd come nearest to giving credence to the report they'd heard so briefly on the radio.

"H-hello," he said, a bit weakly.

"Hi, Mack," said the Martian on the lamp. "Listen, you better throw that hand of yours away after the draw."

"Huh?"

"I'm telling you, Mack. Sevens and threes you got there, and you're going to have a full house because the top card on the deck's a seven."

The other Martian said, "That's straight, Mack. And you'd lose your shirt on that full because *this* slob—" He pointed to Harry Wainright, who had opened the pot. "—opened on three jacks and the fourth jack is the second card from the top of the deck. He'll have four of them."

"Just play the hand out and see," said the first Martian.

Harry Wainright stood up and slammed his cards down face up on the table, three jacks among them. He reached over and took the deck from Trimble, faced the top two cards. They were a seven and a jack. As stated.

"Did you think we were kidding you, Mack?" asked the first Martian.

"Why, you lousy—" The muscles of Wainright's

shoulders bunched under his shirt as he started for the nearest Martian.

"Don't!" George Keller said. "Harry, remember the radio. You can't throw them out if you can't touch them."

"That's right, Mack," said the Martian. "You'll just make a worse ass out of yourself than you are already."

The other Martian said, "Why don't you get back to the game? We'll help all of you, every hand."

Trimble stood up. "You take that one, Harry," he said grimly. "I'll take this one. If the radio was right we can't throw them out, but damned if it'll hurt to try."

It didn't hurt to try. But it didn't help either.

6

Human casualties in all countries that night—or, in the opposite hemisphere, that day—were highest among the military.

At all military installations sentries used their guns. Some challenged and then fired; most of them just fired, and kept on firing until their guns were empty. The Martians jeered and egged them on.

Soldiers who didn't have guns at hand ran to get them. Some got grenades. Officers used their side arms.

All with the result that carnage was terrific, among the soldiers. The Martians got a big bang out of it.

And the greatest mental torture was suffered by the officers in charge of really *top secret* military installations. Because quickly or slowly, according to how smart they were, they realized that there no longer *were* any secrets, top or otherwise. Not from the Martians. Not, since the Martians loved to tattle, from anyone else.

Not that, except for the sake of causing trouble, they had any interest in military matters per se. In fact, they were not in the slightest degree impressed by their examination of secret armed-rocket launching sites, secret A- and H-bomb stock piles, secret files and secret plans.

"Peanut stuff, Mack," one of them sitting on the

desk of a two-star general in charge of Base Able (up to then our really top military secret) told the general. "Peanut stuff. You couldn't lick a tribe of Eskimos with everything you got if the Eskimos knew how to vahr. And we might teach them to, just for the hell of it."

"What the hell is vahring?" roared the general.

"None of your Goddam business, Mack." The Martian turned to one of the other Martians in the room; there were four of them altogether. "Hey," he said, "let's kwim over and take a look at what the Russkies got. And compare notes with them."

He and the other Martian vanished.

"Listen to this," one of the two remaining Martians said to the other. "This is a real boff." And he started reading aloud from a supersecret document in a locked safe in the corner.

The other Martian laughed scornfully.

The general laughed too, although not scornfully. He kept on laughing until two of his aides led him away quietly.

The Pentagon was a madhouse, and so was the Kremlin, although neither building, it must be said, drew more than its proportionate share of Martians, either at the time of their arrival or at any time thereafter.

The Martians were as impartial as they were ubiquitous. No one place or type of place interested them more than did another. White House or cathouse, it didn't matter.

They were no more or less interested in big things like, say, the installations in New Mexico where the space station was being worked on than they were in the details of the sex life of the humblest coolie in Shanghai. They sneered equally at both.

And everywhere and in every way they invaded privacy. Privacy, did I say? There no longer was such a thing.

And it was obvious, even that first night, that for as long as they stayed there would *be* no more privacy, no more secrecy, either in the lives of individuals or in the machinations of nations.

Everything concerning us, individually or collectively, interested them—and amused and disgusted them.

Obviously the proper study of Martiankind was man. Animals, as such, did not interest them, although they did not hesitate to frighten or tease animals whenever such action would have the indirect effect of annoying or injuring human beings.

Horses, in particular, were afraid of them and horseback riding, either for sport or as a means of transportation, became so dangerous as to be impossible.

Only a foolhardy person, while the Martians were with us, dared try to milk a cow that was not firmly secured with its feet tied down and its head in a stanchion.

Dogs became frenetic; many bit their masters and had to be put away.

Only cats, each after an initial experience or two, became used to them and took them calmly and with aplomb. But then cats have always been different.

PART TWO

LANDSCAPE WITH MARTIANS

1

THE MARTIANS stayed, and no one knew or could guess how long they might stay. For all we knew, they might be here permanently. It was none of our business.

And little if anything was learned about them beyond what was obvious within a day or two after their arrival.

Physically, they were pretty much alike. Although not identical, they averaged considerably less physical variation from one of them to another than human beings, of the same race and sex, average.

The only important difference among them was a difference in size; the largest among them was as tall as three feet and the smallest as short as two feet, three inches.

There were several schools of thought, among human beings, as to the explanation of this difference in height among them. Some people thought that they were all adult males—which, judging from their faces, they appeared to be—and that variation in height among them was as natural among them as is variation in height among human beings.

Other people thought that the difference in height indicated a difference in age; that probably they were all adult males but that, with them, growth did not cease at adulthood and that the short ones were relatively young and the tall ones relatively old.

Still other people thought that the tall ones were probably males and the shorter ones females, and that sex differences between them, whatever they might be, didn't show except in height when they had their clothes on. And since no one ever saw a Martian with his clothes off, this possibility, like the others, could be neither proved nor disproved.

And then there was the theory that all Martians were alike sexually, being either bisexual or having no sex at all, as we understand sex, and that possibly they reproduced by parthenogenesis or some means we couldn't even guess at. For all we knew they grew on trees like coconuts and dropped off when they were ripe, already adult and intelligent, ready to face their world, or to face and sneer at ours. In that case, the smallest among them could have been babies, as it were, just off the tree but fully as hateful as the bigger and older ones. If the smallest among them weren't infants, then we never saw a Martian infant.

We never learned what they ate or drank or even whether they did eat or drink. They couldn't have eaten Earth food, of course; they couldn't even pick it up or handle it, for the same reason that we couldn't handle them. Most people thought that, since their kwimming seemed to be an instantaneous process, a Martian would simply kwim to Mars and back again any time he felt the need for food or drink. Or for sleep, if Martians slept, since no one had ever seen a Martian sleeping on Earth.

We knew amazingly little about them.

We didn't know for sure that they were really *here* in person. Many people, and especially scientists, insisted that a life form that is noncorporeal, without solidity, cannot possibly exist. And that therefore what we saw weren't the Martians themselves but *projections* of them, that the Martians had bodies as solid as ours and left their bodies back on Mars, possibly in a trance state, that kwimming was simply the ability to project an astral body that was visible but not corporeal.

If true, that theory explained a lot, but that there was one thing it didn't explain even its most ardent proponents had to admit. How could a noncorporeal projection talk? Sound is the physical movement or vibration of air or other molecules so how could a mere projection that wasn't really there create a sound?

And they certainly created sounds. Actual sounds, not just in the mind of the listener; the fact that the sounds they made could be recorded on wax or tape was proof of that. They could really talk and they could also (but seldom did) knock on doors. The Martian who knocked on Luke Devereaux's door on what came to be called Coming Night had been an exception in that particular respect. Most of them had kwimmed their way, without knocking, right into living rooms, bedrooms, television stations, night clubs, theaters, taverns (there must have been some wonderful scenes in taverns that night), barracks, igloos, jails, everywhere.

They also showed clearly on photographs, as Luke Devereaux would have found out had he ever bothered to have that roll of film developed. Whether they were there or not, they were opaque to light. But not to radar, and scientists tore their hair over that.

They all insisted that they had no names, or even numbers, and that names were ridiculous and unnecessary. None of them ever addressed a human being by name. In the United States they called every man *Mack* and every woman *Toots;* elsewhere they used local equivalents.

In one field at least they showed tremendous aptitude—linguistics. Luke's Martian hadn't been bragging when he said he could learn a new language in an hour or so. The Martians who appeared among various primitive peoples whose tongues had never been broadcast by radio arrived without knowing a word of the language, but they were speaking it adequately within an hour, fluently within a few hours. And whatever language they spoke, they spoke it idiomatically, even slangily, with none of the stiffness and awkwardness with which human beings speak a new language which they have recently acquired.

Many words in their vocabulary were obviously *not* learned from radio broadcasts. But that isn't difficult to account for; within seconds of their arrival they, or many of them, had plenty of opportunity to pick up a liberal education in profanity. The Martian, for example, who had broken up *Romeo and Juliet* on television with his vulgar comment on Romeo's balcony scene speech was no doubt one who had first kwimmed into, say, a tavern but had sought greener pastures within a matter of seconds when he had found too many others of his kind had kwimmed into the same place.

Mentally, the Martians were even more alike than they were physically, although again there was minor variation—some of them were even worse than others.

But one and all they were abusive, aggravating, annoying, brash, brutal, cantankerous, caustic, churlish, detestable, discourteous, execrable, fiendish, flippant, fresh, galling, hateful, hostile, ill-tempered, insolent, impudent, jabbering, jeering, knavish killjoys. They were leering, loathsome, malevolent, malignant, nasty, nauseating, objectionable, peevish, perverse, quarrelsome, rude, sarcastic, splenetic, treacherous, truculent, uncivil, ungracious, waspish, xenophobic, yapping, and zealous in making themselves obnoxious to and in making trouble for everyone with whom they came in contact.

2

Alone again and feeling blue—there wasn't even a Martian present or he'd have felt bluer—Luke Devereaux took his time unpacking two suitcases in the little room in a cheap rooming house he'd just taken in Long Beach.

It was just two weeks after Coming Night. Luke had fifty-six dollars left between himself and starvation and he'd come to Long Beach to look for a job, any kind of job that would keep him eating after that fifty-six dollars was gone. He'd given up even trying to write, for a while.

He'd been lucky in one way, very lucky. He'd been able to sublet his hundred-dollars-a-month Hollywood bachelor apartment, which he'd furnished himself, for the same figure by renting it furnished. That left him free to cut his living expenses and still hang onto the bulk of his possessions without having to pay storage on them. He couldn't have sold them for enough to bother about anyway because the most expensive items were his television set and his radio, and both of those were utterly worthless at the present moment. If the Martians ever left, they'd be valuable again.

So here he was in the cheapest district of Long Beach and all he'd brought with him were two suitcases of clothes and his portable typewriter, the latter for writing letters of application.

He'd probably have to write plenty of them, he thought gloomily. Even here in Long Beach the situation was going to be tough. In Hollywood it would have been impossible.

Hollywood was the hardest hit spot in the country. Hollywood, Beverly Hills, Culver City and the whole movie colony area. Everybody connected in whatever capacity with the movie and television and radio businesses was out of work. Actors, producers, announcers, everyone. All in the same boat, and the boat had sunk suddenly.

And by secondary reaction everything else in Hollywood was being hit hard. Bankrupt or failing were the thousands of shops, beauty parlors, hotels, taverns, restaurants and call houses whose clientele had been mostly among movie people.

Hollywood was becoming a deserted village. The only people staying there were those who, for one reason or another, couldn't get out. As he, Luke, wouldn't have been able to get out, except by walking, if he'd waited much longer.

Probably, he thought, he should have gone farther from Hollywood than Long Beach but he hated to cut deeply into his dwindling hoard for long-distance transportation. And anyway, things were tough all over.

Throughout the country—except Hollywood, which simply gave up—BUSINESS AS USUAL had been the slogan for a week now.

And in some businesses it worked, more or less. You can get used to driving a truck with a Martian sneering at the way you drive or jumping up and down on the hood—or if you can't get used to it, at least you can *do* it. Or you can sell groceries across a counter with a Martian sitting—weightlessly but irremovably—on top of your head and dangling his feet in front of your face while he heckles you and the customer impartially. Things like that are wearing on the nerves but they can be done.

Other businesses did not fare so well. As we have seen, the entertainment business was the first and hardest hit.

Live television was particularly impossible. Although filmed television shows were not interrupted that first night, except at some stations where technicians panicked at the sight of Martians, every live television broadcast was off the air within minutes. The Martians *loved* to disrupt live broadcasts, either television or radio ones.

Some television and radio stations closed down completely, for the duration, or forever if the Martians stayed forever. Others were still operating, using only canned material, but it was obvious that people would tire soon of seeing and hearing old material over and over again—even when a temporary absence of Martians in the living room permitted them to see and hear it without interruption.

And, of course, no one in his right mind was interested in buying *new* television and radio sets, so there went a good many more thousands of people out of work all over the country, all of those engaged in the manufacture and sale of television and radio sets.

And the many thousands who had worked in theaters, concert halls, stadiums, other places of mass entertainment. Mass entertainment of any sort was out; when you brought together a mass of people you brought together a mass of Martians, and whatever was supposed to be entertainment ceased to be such even if it was possible for it to continue at all. Scratch baseball players, ticket sellers, ushers, wrestlers, projectionists . . .

Yes, things were tough all over. The Great Depression of the nineteen thirties was beginning to look like a period of prosperity.

Yes, Luke was thinking, it was going to be a tough job to find a job. And the sooner he got at it the better. He tossed the last few things impatiently into the dresser drawer, noticing somewhat to his surprise that Margie's Y.W.C.A. T-shirt was among them—why had he brought that?—felt his face to remind himself that he'd shaved, ran his pocket comb quickly through his hair, and left the room.

The telephone was on a table in the hall and he sat down at it and pulled the phone book over. Two Long Beach newspapers came first. Not that he had any real hope of getting on one, but reporting was the least onerous type of work he could think of, and it wouldn't cost him anything to try, except for a couple of dimes in the telephone. Besides he knew Hank Freeman on the *News*, which might give him an in on one of the two papers.

He dialed the *News*. There was a Martian at the switchboard jabbering along with the switchboard girl, trying to foul up calls and sometimes succeeding, but he finally got through to Hank. Hank worked on the city desk.

"Luke Devereaux, Hank. How are things?"

"Wonderful, if you don't care what you say. How are the Greenies treating you, Luke?"

"No worse than anybody else, I guess. Except that I'm looking for a job. How are chances of getting on the *News*?"

"Zero point zero. There's a waiting list as long as your arm for every kind of job here. Plenty of 'em with newspaper experience, too—left newspaper work to go into radio or TV. You never worked on a newspaper, did you?"

"I carried a route when I was a kid."

"You couldn't even get a job doing *that* now, pal. Sorry, there isn't a ghost of a chance of anything, Luke. Things are so tough we're all taking pay cuts.

And with so much high-powered talent trying to get in, I'm afraid of losing my own job."

"Pay cuts? With no competition from newscasts, I'd think newspapers would be booming."

"Circulation is booming. But a newspaper's revenue depends on advertising, not on circulation. And that's way down. So many people are out of work and not buying that every store in town's had to cut its advertising budget with a dull ax. Sorry, Luke."

Luke didn't bother to phone the other newspaper.

He went out, walked over to Pine Avenue and south into the business district. The streets were full of people—and Martians. The people were mostly glum and silent, but the strident voices of the Martians made up for that. There was less auto traffic than usual and most drivers drove very cautiously; Martians had a habit of kwimming suddenly onto the hoods of cars, right in front of windshields. The only answer to that was to drive slowly and with a foot on the brake pedal ready to stop the instant vision was cut off.

It was dangerous, too, to drive *through* a Martian, unless you were sure that he wasn't standing in front of some obstacle to block your view of it.

Luke saw an example of that. There was a line of Martians part way across Pine Avenue just south of Seventh Street. They seemed to be very quiet, for Martians, and Luke wondered why—until a Cadillac came along at about twenty miles an hour and the driver, with a grim look on his face, suddenly speeded up and swerved slightly to drive through the line. It had been masking a two-foot-wide trench dug for laying sewer pipe. The Cadillac bounced like a bronco and the right front wheel came off and rolled ahead of it down Pine Avenue. The driver broke the windshield with his head and got out of the wrecked car dripping blood and profanity. The Martians yelled with glee.

At the next corner, Luke bought a newspaper. And, seeing a shoeshine stand, decided to get a shine while he looked at the ads. His last paid-for shine until after he was solvent and working again, he told himself; hereafter he'd keep his own shoes shined.

He turned to the want ads, looked for MALE HELP WANTED. At first he thought there weren't any such ads, then he found a quarter of a column of them. But there might as well have been none, he realized within a few minutes, as far as he was concerned. Jobs offered were in two categories only—highly skilled technical jobs demanding a special training and experience, and NO EXPERIENCE NEEDED sucker ads for house-to-house canvassers on straight commission. Luke had tried that toughest of rackets years before when he was in his twenties and just getting a start at writing; he'd convinced himself that he couldn't even give away free samples, let alone sell anything. And that had been in "good times." No use his trying it again now, no matter how desperate he got.

Folding back the paper to the front page, he wondered if he'd made a mistake in picking Long Beach. Why *had* he? Not, certainly, because the mental hospital his ex-wife Margie worked at was here. He wasn't going to look her up; he was through with women. For a long time, anyway. A brief but very unpleasant scene with the fair Rosalind the day after his return to Hollywood had shown him that the Martian hadn't been lying about what had happened in her apartment the night before. (Damn them, they never lied when they tattled; you *had* to believe them.)

Had Long Beach been a mistake?

The front page of the paper told him that things were tough all over. DRASTIC CUT IN DEFENSE SPENDING, the President announced. Yes, he admitted that that would cause more unemployment, but the money was desperately needed for relief and would go farther that way. And relief—with people starving—was certainly more important than defense spending, the President told the press conference.

In fact, defense spending wasn't important at all, just at the moment. The Russians and the Chinese were having troubles of their own, worse than ours. Besides, by now we knew all their secrets and they knew all ours—and, the President had said with a wry smile, you can't fight a war *that* way.

Luke, who had served a three-year hitch as an ensign in the navy ten years before, shuddered at the thought of fighting a war with the Martians gleefully helping both sides.

STOCK MARKET STILL ON TOBOGGAN, another article told him. But entertainment stocks, like radio, moving pictures, television and theater, had staged a slight comeback. After being considered completely worthless the week before, they were now being bid for at about a tenth of their former value, as a longshot long range gamble, by people who thought and hoped that the Martians might not stay long. But industrials reflected the defense spending cut with a sharp drop, and all other stocks were down at least a few points. The big drops, all down the line, had happened the week before.

Luke paid for his shine and left the paper on the seat.

A line of men, and a few women, that led around a corner caused him to turn the corner to see where the line led. It was an employment agency. For a moment he considered going back and joining the line; then, in the window, he saw a sign that read REGISTRATION FEE $10, and decided the hell with it. With hundreds of people being registered the chance of getting a job through that agency certainly wasn't worth ten bucks of his dwindling capital. But hundreds of people were paying it.

And if there were any employment agencies that didn't charge registration fees, they'd be mobbed even worse.

He drifted on.

A tall elderly man with fierce eyes and a wild gray beard stood on a soapbox at the curb between two parked cars. Half a dozen people stood listening listlessly. Luke stopped and leaned against a building.

". . . and *why*, I ask you, do they never tell lies in their meddling? *Why* are they truthful? *Why*? So that, since they tell no small lies, you will believe their BIG LIE!

"And what, my friends, is their BIG LIE? *It is, that they are Martians*. That is what they want you to believe, to the eternal damnation of your souls.

"Martians! They are DEVILS, devils out of the foulest depths of hell, sent by SATAN, as is predicted in the Book of Revelations!

"And, O my friends, you are damned, damned unless you see the TRUTH and pray, on your bended knees every hour of the day and night, to the ONE BEING who can drive them back whence they came to tempt and torment us. O my friends, pray to GOD and to His Son, ask forgiveness for the EVILS of the WORLD that loosed these demons . . ."

Luke drifted on.

Probably, he thought, all over the world religious fanatics were taking that line, or a similar one.

Well, they could even be right. There wasn't any proof that they were Martians. Only thing was, he personally believed that there *could* be Martians and he didn't believe in devils and demons at all. For that reason, he was willing to take the Martians' word for it.

Another queue, another employment agency.

A boy walking along with a pile of handbills handed Luke one. He slowed down to glance at it.

"GREAT OPPORTUNITIES IN NEW PROFESSION," he read. "BECOME A PSYCHOLOGICAL CONSULTANT."

The rest was in smaller type and he stuffed it into his pocket. Maybe he'd read it later. A new racket, probably. A depression breeds rackets as a swamp breeds mosquitoes.

Another line of people leading around a corner. It seemed longer than the two other lines he'd passed and he wondered if it might be a public employment agency, one that wouldn't charge a registration fee.

If so, it wouldn't hurt to register, since he couldn't think of anything more constructive to do at the moment. Besides, if his money ran out before he got a job, he'd have to be registered there before they'd let him go on relief. Or even get on any of the WPA-type projects that the government was already getting ready to organize. Would there be a Writers' Project this time? If so, he could certainly qualify for that, and it wouldn't take creative writing, just boondoggling along on something like a history of Long Beach, and even if he was burned out as a writer he could do that. In his sleep.

And the line seemed to be moving fairly fast, so fast that he decided they must be just handing out blanks for people to fill out and mail in.

Just the same, he'd check the head of the line first and make sure that was what was going on.

It wasn't.

The line led to an emergency soup kitchen. It led through a doorway into a big building that looked as though it had once been a skating rink or a dance hall. It was filled now with long tables improvised from planks laid over sawbucks; hundreds of people, mostly men but a few women, sat at the tables hunched over bowls of soup. Scores of Martians ran up and down the tables, frequently stepping—but without other than visual effect, of course—into the steaming bowls and playing leapfrog over the diners' heads.

The odor of the soup wasn't bad, and it reminded Luke that he was hungry; it must be at least noon and he'd skipped breakfast. Why shouldn't he join the line and husband his dwindling financial resources? Nobody seemed to be asking any questions; anybody who joined the line got a bowl.

Or did they? For a moment, he watched the table on which stood a big kettle of soup, from which a big man in a greasy apron ladled soup into bowls; he noticed that quite a few people turned down the bowl offered them and, with a slightly sickish or disgusted look on their faces, turned and headed out again.

Luke put his hand on the arm of a man walking past him after declining a bowl. "What's the matter?" he asked. "The soup look that bad? It smells all right."

"Go look, chum," said the man, disengaging his arm and hurrying outside.

Luke stepped closer and looked. There was a Martian, he could see now, sitting or squatting in the middle of the bowl of soup. Every few seconds he would bend forward and stick a tremendously long chartreuse tongue into the soup in front of him. Then he'd pull his tongue back and pretend to spit out the soup, making a very disgusted and very disgusting noise in the process. The big man with the ladle paid no attention, dipping soup right out through the Martian. Some of the people in the line—the ones who'd been here before, Luke suspected—paid no attention either, or walked past with eyes carefully averted.

Luke watched a minute longer and then went outside. He didn't join the line. He knew perfectly well that the Martian's presence in it had no effect whatsoever on the soup. But just the same, he wasn't that hungry yet, and wouldn't be while his money lasted.

He found a little five-stool diner, empty of customers and, for the moment at least, also happily empty of Martians. He ate a hamburger sandwich and then ordered another one and a cup of coffee.

He'd finished the second sandwich and was sipping at the coffee when the counterman, a tall blond kid of about nineteen said, "Let me hot it up for you," and took the cup to the coffee urn, filled it and brought it back.

"Thanks," Luke said.

"Want a piecea pie?"

"Uh—I guess not."

"Blueberry pie. It's on the house."

"At that price," Luke said, "sure. But how come?"

"Boss is closing up the place tonight. We got more pie than we'll sell by then. So why not?"

He put a slab of pie and a fork in front of Luke.

"Thanks," Luke said. "Is business really that bad?"

"Brother, things are tough," said the counterman.

3

Brother, things were tough. Nowhere tougher than in the fields of crime and law enforcement. Offhand, you'd say that if things were tough for the cops they'd be good for the crooks, or vice versa, but it didn't work out that way at all.

Things were tough for the forces of law and order because crimes of passion and sudden violence were up, way up. People's nerves were already wearing thin. Since it did no good to attack or quarrel with Martians—or even to *try* to attack or quarrel with them— people quarreled with and fought with one another. Street fights and domestic fights were a dime a dozen. Murders—not the premeditated variety but ones committed in sudden anger or temporary insanity—were two bits a dozen. Yes, the police had their hands full and their jails even fuller.

But if the cops were overworked, professional criminals were underworked, and hungry. Crimes for gain, whether of stealth or violence, *planned* crimes, were down, way down.

The Martians tattled so.

Take, for random but typical example, what happened to Alf Billings, Cockney pickpocket, right while Luke Devereaux was eating his lunch in the Long Beach diner. It was early evening, of course, in London. Let's let Alf tell it in his own words.

67

Take it, Alf.

"Well, Guv'nor, 'ere Hi am fresh from a moon in a flowery, and Hi'm poppin' out of an oozer after a pig's ear that took my last smash. Blimey, Hi'm on the rib. So when I gets a decko at this connaught ranger takin' a pen'worth of chalk down the frog lookin' like 'e'd 'ave a dummy full of bees and honey,'e looks ripe for a buzz. Hi takes a decko around—no bogies. Hi see a greenie on a jam-pot near but 'ow'd Hi know 'e was a grass? Hi *got* to speel or there's no weeping willow for my Uncle Ned. So I closes up and uses my fork to blag—"

Wait, Alf. Maybe you'd better let *me* tell what happened, in *my* words.

Here was little Alf Billings, fresh from a month in jail, coming out of a pub after just having spent his last change for a glass of beer. So when he saw a prosperous-looking stranger walking down the street, he decided to pick his pocket. Nobody in sight looked like a policeman or detective. True, there was a Martian sitting on top of a parked automobile nearby, but Alf hadn't learned much about the Martians yet. And, in any case, Alf was flat broke; he had to take a chance or he wouldn't be able to afford a place to sleep that night. So he closed up on the man and picked his pocket.

That's what Alf just told you, but I thought it better to repeat. And to go on from there:

Suddenly there was the Martian on the sidewalk beside Alf, pointing to the wallet in Alf's hand and chanting delightedly, "Yah, yah, yah, yah, yah, look 'oo blagged a dummy!"

"Nark it, you bloody barstard," Alf growled, shoving the wallet quickly out of sight into his own pocket and turning to slouch away.

But the Martian didn't nark it. He kept pace with poor Alf, and kept up his delighted chanting. And with a quick look over his shoulder, Alf saw that his victim had turned, was feeling in his hip pocket and getting set to start after Alf and his little companion.

Alf ran. Around the nearest corner and right into the blue-clad arms of a bobby.

You see what I mean.

It wasn't that the Martians were against crime or criminals, except in the sense that they were against everything and everybody. They loved to make trouble and catching a criminal either planning a crime or in the act of committing one gave them such a beautiful opportunity.

But once a criminal was caught, they were equally assiduous in heckling the police. In court they would drive judges, lawyers, witnesses and juries to such distraction that there were more mistrials than completed ones. With Martians in a courtroom, Justice would have had to be deaf as well as blind in order to ignore them.

4

"Damn good pie," Luke said, putting down his fork. "Thanks again."

"More coffee?"

"No, thanks. I've had plenty."

"Nothin' else at all?"

Luke grinned. "Sure, a job."

The tall young man had been leaning both hands on the counter. He suddenly straightened. "Say, that's an idea, brother. Would you take one for half a day? From now til five o'clock?"

Luke stared at him. "You serious? Sure I would. Better than wasting the afternoon looking for one."

"Then you got yourself one." He came around from behind the counter, pulling his apron off as he came. "Hang up your coat and put this on." He tossed the apron on the counter.

"Okay," said Luke, not yet reaching for the apron. "But what's it all about? What's the score?"

"I'm heading for the hills, that's the score." And then at the expression on Luke's face, he grinned. "All right. I'll tell you all about it. But let's introduce ourselves. I'm Rance Carter." He stuck out his hand.

Luke said "Luke Devereaux," and shook it.

Rance sat down on a stool, one stool away so they could face one another. He said, "Wasn't kidding about being a hillbilly; anyway I was one till two years ago when I came to California. Paw and maw got a little farm—bottom land, too—near Hartville, Missouri. Wasn't satisfied there then, but with what's happenin' now—and me outa work fer God knows how long, reckon I shore want back there now." His eyes were shining with excitement—or homesickness—and with every sentence his accent slipped farther and farther back into the hillbilly.

Luke nodded. "Good idea. At least you'll eat. And there'll be fewer Martians around a farm than in a city."

"You said it. Made up muh mind tuh go back soon as the boss said he was closin' up. Sooner the better and I been gettin' in a hellfire hurry all mornin' and your askin' about a job give me an idea. Promised the boss I'd keep the place open tell five uh-clock—when he gets down—an' guess I'm too damn honest tuh jest close up an' walk out on him. But it cain't make no deffrence ef I let you do it instead, can it?"

"I guess not," said Luke. "But will he pay me?"

"I'll pay you. Get ten a day besides mah eats, an' I'm paid through yesterday. Ten bucks comin' for today. I'll take it out uh the register an' leave a note, give you five bucks an' keep five bucks."

"Fair enough," said Luke. "It's a deal." He stood up, peeling off his suit coat, and hung it on one of the hooks on the wall. He put the apron on, tied the cords.

Rance had put on his own suit coat and was at the register back of the counter, taking out two five dollar bills.

"Cal-eye-for-nee, here Ah go—" he caroled, and then paused, obviously at a loss for a second line.

"Right back home to Hartville, Mo!" Luke supplied.

Rance stared at him in open-mouthed admiration. "Hey, guy, did you think uh that jest like *that*?" He snapped his fingers. "Say, you oughta be a writer, or somethin'."

"I'll settle for being something," Luke told him. "By the way, anything I should know about this job?"

"Nah. Prices are on the wall there. Everything that ain't in sight's in the 'frigerator there. Here's the five and thanks to hell and back."

"Good luck," said Luke. They shook hands and Rance went out singing happily, "Cal-eye-for-nee, here Ah go—right back home to . . ."

Luke spent ten minutes familiarizing himself with the contents of the refrigerator and the prices on the wall. Ham and eggs looked to be the most complicated thing he might have to prepare. And he'd done that often enough for himself at home. Any writer who is a bachelor and hates to interrupt himself to go out to eat becomes a fairly good short order cook.

Yes, the job looked easy and he hoped the boss would change his mind about closing the place. Ten bucks a day, with his meals furnished as well, would be plenty for him to get along on for a while. And with the pressure off maybe he could even start writing again, evenings.

But business, or the lack of it, killed that hope long before the afternoon was over. Customers came in at the rate of about one an hour and usually spent forty cents or less apiece. A hamburger and coffee for forty cents or pie and coffee for thirty-five. One plunger brought the average up a little by shooting ninety-five cents for a hamburger steak, but it was obvious, even to a nonbusinessman like Luke, that the take wasn't covering the cost of food plus overhead, even if his own pay was the only item of overhead involved.

Several times Martians kwimmed into the place, but, as it happened, never while a customer was eating at the counter. Finding Luke alone, none of them tried to do anything seriously annoying and none stayed longer than a few minutes.

At a quarter of five Luke wasn't hungry again as yet but decided he might as well save a little money by stocking up for the evening. He made himself a boiled ham sandwich and ate it. Made himself another, wrapped it and put it into the pocket of his coat hanging on the wall.

As he put it there his hand encountered a folded paper, the handbill that had been given to him on the street earlier in the day. He took it back to the counter and unfolded it to read while he had a final cup of coffee.

"BEAT THE DEPRESSION

WITH A NEW PROFESSION," the handbill told him. And in smaller type, "Become a Consulting Psychologist."

Neither heading was in flagrantly large type. And the body type was ten-point Bodoni with wide margins; the effect as a whole was very conservative and pleasing for a handbill.

"Are you intelligent, presentable, well-educated—but unemployed?" the handbill asked him. Luke almost nodded a yes before he read on.

If you are, there is an opportunity now for you to help humanity, and yourself, by becoming a consulting psychologist, by advising people how to remain calm and to stay sane despite the Martians, for however long they stay.

If you are properly qualified, and especially if you already have a fair lay knowledge of psychology, a very few lessons, perhaps as few as two or three, will give you sufficient knowledge and insight to help first yourself and then others to withstand the concerted attack upon human sanity which is being made by the Martians today.

Classes will be limited to seven persons, to permit free discussion and the asking of questions after each class. The fee will be very moderate, five dollars per lesson.

Your instructor will be the undersigned, Bachelor of Science (Ohio State, 1953), Doctor of Psychology (U.S.C., 1958), subsequently with five years' experience as an industrial psychologist with Convair Corporation, active member of American Association of Psychologists, author of several monographs and of one book *You and Your Nerves*, Dutton, 1962.

RALPH S. FORBES, PS.D.

And a Long Beach telephone number.

Luke read it again before he folded it and put it in his pocket. It didn't sound like a racket—not if the guy really had those qualifications.

And it made sense. People *were* going to need help, and need it badly; they were cracking up right and left. If Doc Forbes had even a piece of the answer—

He glanced at the clock and saw that it was ten minutes after five, and was wondering how late "the boss" might be, and whether or not he should just lock the door and leave, when the door opened.

The middle-aged stocky man who came in looked at Luke sharply. "Where's Rance?"

"On his way back to Missouri. You the owner?"

"Yeah. What happened?"

Luke explained. The owner nodded and came around the counter. He opened the register, read Rance's note, and grunted. He counted the cash in the register—it didn't take long—and pulled a strip of paper out of the side to check the reading on it. He granted again and turned back to Luke.

"Business really that lousy?" he asked. "Or did you drag down a few bucks?"

"Business was really that lousy," Luke told him. "If I'd taken in even ten bucks I might have been tempted. But not when I took in less than five. That's less than my minimum price for being crooked."

The owner sighed. "Okay, I believe you. Had your dinner?"

"Had a sandwich. And put another in my pocket."

"Hell, make a few more. Enough to last you tomorrow. I'm going to close up now—what's the use of wasting an evening?—and take home what grub's left. But it's more'n my wife and I can eat before it starts to spoil."

"Thanks, guess I might as well," Luke said.

He made himself three more cold sandwiches and, when he left, took them along; they'd save him from having to spend money for food for another day.

Back in his room, he carefully locked the sandwiches in the tightest closing one of his suitcases to protect them from mice and cockroaches—if there were mice or cockroaches around; he hadn't seen any yet, but he'd just taken the room that morning.

He took the handbill from his pocket to read it again. Suddenly a Martian was perched on his shoulder reading it with him. The Martian finished first, howled with laughter, and was gone.

It made sense, that handbill. At least enough sense to make him want to gamble five dollars on *one* lesson from the psychology prof. He took out his wallet and counted his money again. Sixty-one dollars; five more than he'd had left after paying a week's room rent this morning. Because of his lucky break at the lunch counter, he was not only richer by that five bucks, but he'd had to spend no money on food today nor would he have to spend any tomorrow.

Why not gamble that five bucks and see if he could

parlay it into a steady income? Hell, even if he never followed through and made any money out of it, he might get five bucks' worth of information on how to control his own temper and his own reactions towards the Martians. Possibly even to the point where he could try writing again soon.

Before he could weaken and change his mind he went to the telephone in the hall and dialed the number on the handbill.

A calm, resonant male voice identified itself as that of Ralph Forbes.

Luke gave his own name. "I've read your handbill, Doctor," he said, "and I'm interested. When are you holding your next class, and is it filled yet?"

"I haven't given a class yet, Mr. Devereaux. I'm starting my first group this evening at seven, about an hour from now. And another group at two o'clock tomorrow afternoon. Neither group is filled as yet; as it happens I have five reservations for each, so you may have your choice."

"In that case, the sooner the better," Luke said. "So put me down for this evening, please. Are you having these classes at your home?"

"No, I've taken a small office for the purpose. Room six-fourteen in the Draeger Building on Pine Avenue just north of Ocean Boulevard. But just a moment; before you hang up, may I explain something to you and ask a few questions?"

"Go ahead, Doctor."

"Thank you. Before I enroll you I hope you'll forgive my asking a few questions about your background. You see, Mr. Devereaux, this is not a—ah—racket. While I hope to make money from it, naturally, I'm also interested in helping people, and a great many people are going to need a great deal of help. More people than I can hope to advise individually.

That is why I have chosen this method, working through others."

"I see," Luke said. "You're looking for disciples to make into apostles."

The psychologist laughed. "Cleverly put. But let's not carry the analogy any farther—I assure you that I do not consider myself a messiah. But I do have enough humble faith in my ability to help others to make me want to choose my pupils carefully. Especially since I'm keeping my classes so small, I want to be sure to confine my efforts to people who—ah—"

"I understand perfectly," Luke cut in. "Go ahead with the questions."

"Do you have a college education, or equivalent?"

"I went to college two years, but I think I can claim to have the equivalent of a college education—an unspecialized one, that is. I've been an omnivorous reader all my life."

"And how long, may I ask, has that been?"

"Thirty-seven years. Wait, I mean that I'm thirty-seven years old. I haven't been reading *quite* that long, by a few years anyway."

"Have you read much in the field of psychology?"

"Nothing technical. Quite a few of the popular books, the ones written for laymen."

"And what, may I ask, has been your principal occupation?"

"Fiction writing."

"Indeed. *Science* fiction? Are you by any chance *Luke* Devereaux?"

Luke felt the warm glow a writer always feels when his name is recognized. "Yes," he said. "Don't tell me yon read science fiction."

"But I do, and love it. At least I did until two weeks ago. I don't imagine anyone is in the mood to read about extraterrestrials right now. Come to think of it, there must be quite a sharp break in the science-fiction market. Is that why you're looking for a new—ah—profession?"

"I'm afraid that even before the Martians came I was in the worst slump of my writing career, so I can't blame it all on them. Not that they've helped, of course. And you can say what you said about the science-fiction market again and a lot more strongly. There just isn't any such market any more, and there may not be one for years after the Martians leave—if they ever leave."

"I see. Well, Mr. Devereaux, I'm sorry you've run into bad luck with your writing; needless to say, though, I'll be more than glad to have you in one of my classes. If you'd happened to mention your first name as well as your last when you identified yourself a moment ago, I assure you my questions would have been needless. I'll see you at seven this evening, then?"

"Right," Luke said.

Maybe the psychologist's questions had been needless, but Luke was glad he'd asked them. He was sure now that this was not a racket, that the man was everything he claimed to be.

And that the five dollars he was about to spend might be the best investment he'd ever made. He felt certain now that he *was* going to have a new profession, and an important one. He felt sure that he was going to follow through and take as many lessons as Forbes would decide he needed, even if it was more than the two or three that Forbes' advertisement had said might be enough. If his money ran out first, no doubt Forbes—already knowing him by name and admiring him as a writer—would be willing to let him have the last few lessons on credit and let him pay for them after he was making money helping others.

And between lessons he'd spend his time at the public library or reading books taken home from it, not just reading but actually studying every book on psychology he could lay his hands on. He was a fast reader and had a retentive memory, and if he was going in for this thing he might as well do it whole hog and make himself into as near to a real psychologist as it was possible to become without the accolade of a degree. Even that, maybe, someday. Why not? If he was really through as a writer it would be better for him really to shoot, no matter how tough the shooting might be at first, for a foothold in another legitimate profession. He was still young enough, damn it.

He took a quick shower and shaved. Nicking himself slightly when a sudden Bronx cheer sounded right in his ear as he was in the middle of a stroke; there hadn't been a Martian around a second before. It wasn't a deep cut, though, and his styptic pencil stopped the bleeding easily. Could even a psychologist, he wondered, ever become sufficiently conditioned to things like that to avoid the reaction that had made him cut himself? Well, Forbes would know the answer to that. And if there wasn't a better answer, an electric razor would solve the problem. He'd get himself one as soon as he was solvent again.

He wanted his appearance to back up the impression his name had made, so he put on his best suit— the tan gabardine—a clean white shirt, hesitated over the choice between his Countess Mara tie and a more conservative blue one, and chose the blue.

He left, whistling. Walked jauntily, feeling that this was a turning point in his life, the start of a new and better era.

The elevators in the Draeger Building weren't running but it didn't discourage him to have to walk up to the sixth floor; it exhilarated him instead.

As he opened the door of six-fourteen, a tall slender man in Oxford gray, with thick shell-rimmed glasses, rose and came around from behind a desk to shake hands with him. "Luke Devereaux?" he asked.

"Right, Doctor Forbes. But how did you know me?"

Forbes smiled. "Partly by elimination—everyone who's signed up was already here except yourself and one other. And partly because I've seen your picture on a book jacket."

Luke turned and saw that there were four others already in the office, seated in comfortable chairs. Two men and two women. They were all well-dressed and looked intelligent and likeable. And there was one Martian, seated cross-legged on a corner of Forbes' desk, doing nothing but looking bored at the moment. Forbes introduced Luke around—except to the Martian. The men were named Kendall and Brent; the women were a Miss Kowalski and a Mrs. Johnston.

"And I'd introduce you to our Martian friend if he had a name," said Forbes cheerfully. "But they tell us they do not use names."

"——you, Mack," said the Martian.

Luke chose one of the unoccupied chairs and Forbes went back to his swivel chair behind the desk. He glanced at his wristwatch. "Seven exactly," he said. "But I think we should allow a few minutes for our final member to arrive. Do you all agree?"

All of them nodded and Miss Kowalski asked, "Do you want to collect from us now, while we're waiting?"

Five five-dollar bills, including Luke's, were passed up to the desk. Forbes left them lying there, in sight. "Thank you," he said. "I'll leave them there. If any of you is not satisfied when the lesson is over, he may take his money back. Ah, here is our final member. Mr. Gresham?"

He shook hands with the newcomer, a bald middle-aged man who looked vaguely familiar to Luke—although Luke couldn't place the name or where he'd seen him—introduced him around to the other class members. Gresham saw the pile of bills on the desk and added his, then took the vacant seat next to Luke's. While Forbes was arranging some notes in front of him Gresham leaned over toward Luke. "Haven't we met somewhere?" he whispered.

"We must have met," Luke said. "I had the same feeling. But let's compare notes afterwards. Wait, I think I—"

"*Quiet*, please!"

Luke stopped and leaned back abruptly. Then flushed a little when he realized that it was the Martian who had spoken, not Forbes. The Martian grinned at him.

Forbes smiled. "Let me start by saying that you will find it impossible to ignore Martians—especially when they say or do something unexpectedly. I hadn't meant to bring up that point right away, but since it is obvious that I am going to have 'help' in this class tonight, perhaps it is best that I start with a statement which I had intended to lead up to gradually.

"It is this: your life, your thoughts, your sanity—as well as the lives, thoughts and sanity of those whom I hope you will advise and teach—will be least affected by them if you choose the middle way between trying to ignore them completely and letting yourself take them too seriously.

"To ignore them completely—rather, to try to ignore them completely, to pretend that they aren't there when so obviously they are, is a form of rejection of reality that can lead straight to schizophrenia and paranoia. Conversely, to pay full attention to them, to let yourself become seriously angry with them can lead straight to nervous breakdown—or apoplexy."

It made sense, Luke thought. In almost anything, the middle way is the best way.

The Martian on the corner of Forbes' desk yawned mightily.

A second Martian suddenly kwimmed into the room, right in the middle of Forbes' desk. So close to Forbes' nose that he let out an involuntary yip. Then smiled at the class over the Martian's head.

Then he glanced down to look at his notes; the new Martian was sitting on them. He reached a hand through the Martian and slid them to one side; the Martian moved with them.

Forbes sighed and then looked up at the class. "Well, it looks as though I'll have to talk without notes. Their sense of humor is very childlike."

He leaned to one side to see better around the head of the Martian sitting in front of him. The Martian leaned that way, too. Forbes straightened, and so did the Martian.

"Their sense of humor is very childlike," Forbes repeated. "Which reminds me to tell you that it was through the study of children and their reaction to Martians that I have formulated most of my theories. You have all no doubt observed that, after the first few hours, after the novelty wore off, children became used to the presence of Martians much more easily and readily than adults. Especially children under five. I have two children of my own and—"

"Three, Mack," said the Martian on the corner of the desk. "I saw that agreement you gave the dame in Gardena two thousand bucks for, so she wouldn't file a paternity suit."

Forbes flushed. "I have two children *at home,*" he said firmly, "and—"

"And an alcoholic wife," said the Martian. "Don't forget *her.*"

Forbes waited a few moments with his eyes closed, as though silently counting.

"The nervous systems of children," he said, "as I explained in *You And Your Nerves,* my popular book on—"

"Not so damned popular, Mack. That royalty statement shows less than a thousand copies."

"I meant that it was written in popular style."

"Then why didn't it sell?"

"Because people didn't buy it," snapped Forbes. He smiled at the class. "Forgive me. I should not have permitted myself to be drawn into pointless argument. If they ask ridiculous questions, do not answer."

The Martian who had been sitting on his notes suddenly kwimmed into a sitting position atop his head, dangling legs in front of his face and swinging them so his vision was alternately clear and blocked.

He glanced down at his notes, now again visible to him—part of the time. He said, "An—I see I have a notation here to remind you, and I had better do so while I can read the notation, that in dealing with the people whom you are to help, you must be completely truthful—"

"Why weren't *you*, Mack?" asked the Martian on the corner of the desk.

"—and make no unjustified claims about yourself or—"

"Like you did in that circular, Mack? Forgetting to say those several monographs you mention weren't ever published?"

Forbes' face was turning beet red behind its pendulum of green-clad legs. He rose slowly to a standing position, his hands gripping the desk's edge. He said, "I—ah—"

"Or why didn't you tell them, Mack, that you were only an assistant psychologist at Convair, and why they fired you?" And the corner-of-the-desk Martian, put his thumbs in his ears, waggled his other fingers and emitted a very loud and juicy Bronx cheer.

Forbes swung at him, hard. And then screamed in pain as his fist, passing through the Martian, struck and knocked off the desk the heavy metal desk lamp which the Martian had been sitting over and concealing.

He pulled back his injured hand and stared at it blankly through the pendulum of the second Martian's legs. Suddenly, both Martians were gone.

Forbes, his face now white instead of red, sat down slowly and stared blankly at the six people seated in his office, as though wondering why they were there. He brushed his hand across his face as though pushing away something that was no longer there, and which couldn't have been pushed away while it was.

He said, "In dealing with Martians, it is important to remember—"

Then he dropped his head into his arms on the desk in front of him and started sobbing quietly.

The woman who had been introduced as Mrs. Johnston had been seated nearest the desk. She stood up and leaned forward, put her hand on his shoulder. "Mr. Forbes," she said. "Mr. Forbes, are you all right?"

There was no answer except that the sobbing stopped slowly.

All the others were standing now too. Mrs. Johnston turned to them. "I think we'd better leave him," she said. "And—" she picked up the six five-dollar bills. "—I guess we've got these coming back." She kept one and passed the others around. They left, very quietly, some of them walking on tiptoe.

Except for Luke Devereaux and the Mr. Gresham who had sat next to him. "Let's stay," Gresham had said. "He may need help." And Luke had nodded.

Now, with the others gone, they lifted Forbes' head from the desk and held him straight in the chair. His eyes were open but stared at them blankly.

"Shock," Gresham said. "He *may* come out of it and be all right. But—" His voice sounded doubtful.

"Think we'd better send for the men in the white coats?"

Luke had been examining Forbes' injured hand. "It's broken," he said. "He'll need attention for that, anyway. Let's phone for a doctor. If he hasn't come out of it by then, let the doc take the responsibility for having them come and get him."

"Good idea. But maybe we won't have to phone. There's a doctor's office next door. I noticed when I came here, and the light was on. He must either have evening hours or be working late."

The doctor had been working late, and was just leaving when they caught him. They brought him into Forbes' office, explained what had happened, told him it was his responsibility now, and then left.

Going down the stairs, Luke said, "He was a good guy, while he lasted."

"And had a good idea, while *it* lasted."

"Yeah," Luke said. "And I feel lower than a mole's basement. Say, we were going to figure out where we've seen or met one another. Have you remembered?"

"Could it have been at Paramount? I worked there six years up to when they closed two weeks ago."

"That's it," said Luke. "You wrote continuity. I put in a few weeks there a few years ago, on scripts. Didn't do so hot, and quit. What talent I've got is for the written word, not for scripting."

"That's it, then. Say, Devereaux—"

"Make it Luke. And your first name's Steve, isn't it?"

"Right. Well, Luke, I feel lower than a mole's basement, too. And I know how I'm going to spend the five bucks I just got back. Got any idea about yours?"

"The same idea you have. After we buy some, shall we go to my room or yours?"

They compared notes on rooms and decided on

Luke's; Steve Gresham was staying with his sister and her husband; there were children and other disadvantages, so Luke's room would be best.

They drowned their sorrows, drink for drink; Luke turned out to have the better capacity of the two of them. At a little after midnight, Gresham passed out cold; Luke was still operating, if a bit erratically.

He tried and failed to wake up Gresham, then sadly poured himself another drink and sat down with it to drink and think instead of drinking and talking. But he wanted to talk rather than to think and almost, but not quite, wished a Martian would show up. But none did. And he wasn't crazy enough or drunk enough to talk to himself. "Not yet anyway," he said aloud, and the sound of his voice startled him to silence again.

Poor Forbes, he thought. He and Gresham had deserted; they should have stayed with Forbes and tried to see him through, at least until and unless they found out it was hopeless. They hadn't even waited for the doctor's diagnosis. Had the doc been able to snap Forbes out of it, or had he sent for the men in the white coats?

He could phone the doctor and ask him what had happened.

Except that he didn't remember the doctor's name, if he had ever heard it.

He could call Long Beach General Mental Hospital and find out if Forbes had been taken there. Or if he asked for Margie, she could find out for him more about Forbes' condition than the switchboard would tell him. But he didn't want to talk to Margie. Yes, he did. No, he didn't; she divorced him and to hell with her. To hell with all women.

He went out in the hallway to the phone, staggering only slightly. But he had to close one eye to read the fine type in the phone book, and again to dial the number.

He asked for Margie.

"Last name, please?"

"Uh—" For a blank second he couldn't remember Margie's maiden name. Then he remembered it, but decided that she might not have decided to use it again, especially since the divorce wasn't final yet. "Margie Devereaux. Nurse."

"One moment please."

And several moments later, Margie's voice. "Hello."

"Hi, Marge. S'Luke. D'I wake you up?"

"No, I'm on night duty. Luke, I'm glad you called. I've been worried about you."

"Worried 'bout *me*? I'm aw right. Why worry 'bout me?"

"Well—the Martians. So many people are— Well, I've just been worrying."

"Thought they'd send me off my rocker, huh? Don't worry, honey, they can't get me down. Write science fiction, 'member? Wrote it, I mean, I *invented* Martians."

"Are you sure you're all right, Luke? You've been drinking."

"Sure, been drinking. But I'm aw right. How're *you*?"

"Fine. But *awfully* busy. This place is—well it's a madhouse. I can't talk long. Did you want anything?"

"Don't wanna thing, honey. I'm *fine*."

"Then I'll have to hang up. But I do want to talk to you, Luke. Will you phone me tomorrow afternoon?"

"Sure, honey. Wha' time?"

"Any time after noon. 'Bye, Luke."

" 'Bye, honey."

He went back to his drink, suddenly remembering that he'd forgotten to ask Margie about Forbes. Well, the hell with Forbes; it didn't matter. He was either okay or he wasn't, and nothing could be done about it if he wasn't.

Surprising. though, that Margie'd been so friendly. Especially since she'd recognized that he was drunk. She wasn't a prig about drinking—she herself drank moderately. But always got mad at him if he let go and drank too much, like tonight.

Must really have been worried about him. But why?

And then he remembered. She'd always suspected him of not being very stable mentally. Had tried to get him to have analysis once—that was one of the things they'd quarreled about. So naturally now, with so many people going nuts, she'd think him likely to be one of the first to go.

To hell with her, if she thought *that*. He was going to be the last to let the Martians get him down, not the first.

He poured himself another drink. Not that he really wanted it—he was plenty drunk already—but to defy Margie and the Martians. He'd show 'em.

One was in the room now. One Martian, not one Margie.

Luke leveled an unsteady finger at it. "Can't get me down," he said, "I 'nvented you."

"You're already down, Mack. You're drunk as a skunk."

The Martian looked disgustedly from Luke to Gresham, snoring on the bed. And must have decided that neither of them was worth annoying, for it vanished.

"See. Told you so," Luke said.

Took another drink from his glass and then put the glass down just in time, for his chin fell forward on his chest and he slept.

And dreamed of Margie. Part of the time he dreamed of quarreling and fighting with her and part of the time he dreamed—but even while the Martians were around, dreams remained private.

5

The Iron Curtain quivered like an aspen leaf in an earthquake.

The leaders of the People found themselves faced with an internal opposition that they could not purge, could not even intimidate.

And not only could they not blame the Martians on the Capitalist warmongers but they soon found out that the Martians were *worse* than Capitalist warmongers.

Not only were they not Marxists but they would admit to no political philosophy whatsoever and sneered at all of them. They sneered equally at all terrestrial governments and forms of government, even theoretical ones. Yes, they themselves had the perfect form of government but they refused to tell anyone what it was—except that it was none of our business.

They weren't missionaries and had no desire to help us. All they wanted was to know everything that went on and to be as annoying and irritating as they possibly could.

Behind the trembling curtain, they succeeded wonderfully.

How could one tell the Big Lie or even a little one, with a third of a billion Martians gleefully ready to punch holes in it? They loved propaganda.

And they tattled so. No one can guess how many people were summarily tried and executed in Communist countries during the first month or two of the Martians' stay. Peasants, factory superintendents, generals, Politburo members. It wasn't safe to do or say *anything*, with Martians around. And there seemed always to be Martians around.

After a while, of course, that phase of things eased up. It had to. You can't kill everybody, not even everybody outside the Kremlin, if for no other reason than that then the Capitalist warmongers could march in and take over. You can't even send everybody to Siberia; Siberia would hold them all right, but it wouldn't support them.

Concessions *had* to be made; minor variations in opinion had to be permitted. Minor deviations from the party line had to be ignored if not actually winked at. These things were bad enough.

But what was worse was that propaganda, even *internal* propaganda, was impossible. Facts and figures, in speeches or in print, had to be honest. The Martians *loved* it when they found even the slightest misstatement or exaggeration, and told everybody.

How could you run a government that way?

6

But the Capitalist warmongers were having their troubles too. Who wasn't?

Take Ralph Blaise Wendell. Born at the turn of the century and now sixty-four years old. Tall but becoming a little stooped; slender, with thinning gray hair and tired gray eyes. Although it had not seemed a misfortune at the time, he had had the misfortune to have been elected President of the United States in 1960.

Now and until the November elections brought surcease he was president of a country that contained a hundred and eighty million people—and about sixty million Martians.

Now—now being an evening in early May, six weeks after the Coming—he sat alone in his big office, brooding.

Completely alone; there wasn't even a Martian present. Such solitude was not unusual. Alone, or with only his secretary present, he had as good a chance as anyone else of not being bothered. The Martians haunted presidents and dictators no more than they haunted file clerks and baby sitters. They were no respecters of persons; they were no respecters of anything at all.

And now, at least for the moment, he was alone. The day's work finished, but loath to move. Or too tired to move. Tired with the special weariness that comes from the combination of great responsibility and a feeling of utter inadequacy. Tired with defeat.

He thought back bitterly over the past six weeks and of the mess things had become. A depression that made the so-called Great Depression of the thirties look like prosperity beyond the dreams of avarice.

A depression that had started—not with a stock market crash, although that had followed quickly enough—with the sudden loss of employment of millions of people all at once. Almost everyone connected with entertainment; not only the entertainers but stagehands, ticket takers, scrubwomen. Everyone connected in any capacity with professional sports. Everyone connected with the movie industry in any capacity whatsoever. Everyone connected with radio and television except a few technicians to keep transmitters running and to handle the already-filmed or already-taped replays. And a few, a very few, announcers and commentators.

Every orchestra and dance band musician. Shades of Petrillo!

Nobody had guessed how many millions of people had made their living in one way or another, directly or indirectly, from sports and entertainment. Not until they all lost their jobs at once.

And the fall to almost zero of entertainment stocks had set off the stock market crash.

And the depression had pyramided, and was still pyramiding. Automobile production down 87 per cent over the same month a year ago. People, even those who still had jobs and money, weren't buying new cars. People were staying at home. Where was there to go? Sure, some of them had to drive to work and back but for that purpose the old car was plenty good. Who would be silly enough to buy a new one in a depression like this and especially with the used car market glutted with almost-new cars people had been forced to sell? The wonder was not that automobile production was down 87 per cent but that any new cars were being made at all.

And with cars being driven only when necessary—pleasure driving being no longer a pleasure—the oil fields and the refineries were hard hit too. More than half of the filling stations had closed.

Steel and rubber were hit. More unemployment.

Less construction because people had less money and they weren't building. More unemployment.

And the jails! Jammed to overflowing, despite the almost complete disappearance of organized crime. But they'd become jammed before criminals had discovered that their trade was no longer practical. And what to do now with the thousands of people being arrested daily for crimes of violence or desperation?

What to do with the armed forces, with war no longer a possibility—disband them? And increase unemployment by several more million? Just that afternoon he had signed an order that would grant immediate release to any soldier or sailor who could prove that he had either a job waiting for him or sufficient capital to guarantee his not becoming a public charge. But a pitifully small percentage would be able to qualify.

The national debt—the budget—the make-work programs—the army—the budget—the national debt—President Wendell dropped his head in his hands on the desk in front of him and groaned, feeling very old and very futile.

From a corner of the room came an echoing groan, a mocking one. "Hi, Mack," said a voice. "Working overtime again? Want help?"

And a laugh. A nasty laugh.

7

Not *all* business was bad.

Take the psychiatrists. Going crazy trying to keep other people from going crazy.

Take the morticians. With the death rate, due to the increase in deaths from suicide, violence and apoplexy, still several times normal, there was no depression among the coffin stuffers. They were doing big business, despite the increasing trend toward simple burial or cremation without anything that could really be called a funeral. (It was all too easy for Martians to make a farce out of a funeral, and they especially loved to kibitz a minister's eulogy whenever it strayed from strict fact about the virtues of the deceased or glossed over any of his vices. Whether from previous observation, from eavesdropping or from having read hidden letters or records, the Martians who attended funerals were always able to pounce gleefully on any deviation from the truth in a funeral oration. It wasn't always safe even when the loved one was thought to have led a truly blameless life; all too often the mourners learned things about him that shocked them silly.)

Drugstores did a land-office business in the sale of aspirin tablets, sedatives and ear stopples.

But the biggest boom of all was in the industry in which you'd expect the biggest boom to be, the liquor industry.

Since time immemorial alcohol has been man's favorite gateway of escape from the routine vicissitudes of everyday life. Now man's everyday life had little green vicissitudes a thousand times worse than the routine ones had been. Now he _really_ had something to escape from.

Most drinking, of course, was done in homes.

But taverns were still open, and they were crowded in the afternoon and jammed in the evening. In most of them the backbar mirrors were broken as a result of people throwing glasses, bottles, ash trays or what have you at Martians, and the mirrors weren't replaced because if they were they'd be broken again the same way.

But the taverns still operated and people thronged to them. Sure, Martians thronged to them too, even though Martians didn't drink. The owners and frequenters of taverns had found a partial answer—noise level. Juke boxes were kept going at top volume and most taverns had at least two of them. Radios helped add to the din. People who talked had to yell in their neighbors' ears.

Martians could only add to the volume of sound and the volume was already such that addition was practically superfluous.

If you were a solitary drinker (and more and more people were becoming solitary drinkers) you had less chance of being bothered by Martians in a tavern than anywhere else. There might be a dozen of them about but if you stood bellied up to the bar with a glass in your hand and your eyes closed, you could neither see them nor hear them. If, after a while, you opened your eyes and saw them, it didn't matter because they really didn't register.

Yes, taverns were doing all right.

8

Take *The Yellow Lantern* on Pine Avenue in Long
Beach. A tavern like any tavern, but Luke Devereaux
is in it, and it's time we got back to Luke because
something big is about to happen to him.

He's bellied up to the bar, with a glass in his hand.
And his eyes are closed so we can look him over without disturbing him.

Except that he looks a little thinner, there's no great
difference in him since we saw him last, which was
seven weeks ago. He's still clean and neatly shaven.
His clothes are still good and are in good shape, although his suit could use pressing and the wrinkles in
his shirt collar show that he is now doing his own
laundry. But it's a sport shirt and doesn't look too bad.

Let's face it; he's been lucky, until tonight. Lucky
in that he had been able to make his original fifty-six
dollars, supplemented by occasional small earnings,
last him these seven weeks and hasn't had to go on
relief. As yet.

Tomorrow, he had decided, he would.

And he'd made the decision while he still had six
dollars left, and for a very good reason. Since the night
when he'd got drunk with Gresham and had phoned
Margie, he had not had a single, solitary drink. He
had lived like a monk and had toiled like a beaver
whenever he'd found anything to toil at.

For seven weeks his pride had kept him going. (The same pride, incidentally, had kept him from phoning Margie again as he had drunkenly promised to do that night. He'd wanted to, but Margie had a job and he wasn't going to see or even talk to her until and unless he himself had one.)

But tonight after the tenth consecutive completely discouraging day (eleven days ago he'd earned three dollars helping a man move a houseful of furniture) and after paying for a frugal meal of day-old buns and discouraged cold frankfurters to eat in his room, he had counted his dwindling capital and had found it to be exactly six dollars, to the penny.

And had decided to hell with it. Unless a miracle happened, and he thought that no miracle was going to happen, he'd have to give up and go on relief within a few more days in any case. If he decided now to go on relief tomorrow he had enough left for one final binge first. After seven weeks of total abstinence and on a not too full stomach, six dollars was enough to get him plenty drunk even if he spent it all in a tavern. Or if he didn't enjoy the tavern he could spend only part of it there and the rest on a bottle to take back to his room. In either case he'd awaken horribly hung over, but with empty pockets and a clear conscience in going on relief. It would be less unpleasant, probably, with a hang-over than otherwise.

And so, having decided that no miracle could happen to him, he had come to *The Yellow Lantern*, where the miracle awaited him.

Stood at the bar with his fourth drink in front of him and his hand clasped around it. A bit disappointed that he didn't feel the first three drinks more. But there was still money for quite a few more—in his pocket, of course; you don't leave money on a crowded bar and stand in front of it with your eyes closed. And for the same reason, you keep your hand around your glass.

He took another sip from it.

Felt a hand on his shoulder and heard a voice scream, "Luke!" in his ear. The scream could have been a Martian, but not the hand. Somebody here knew him, and he'd wanted to get drunk alone tonight. Damn. Well, he could brush the guy off.

He opened his eyes and turned around.

It was Carter Benson, grinning like a Cheshire cat. Carter Benson, from whom he'd borrowed the use of the shack near Indio where, a couple of months ago, he'd tried to start that science-fiction novel that hadn't got started and never would get started now.

Carter Benson, nice guy, but looking as prosperous as he always looked and probably still in the chips, and the hell with him, tonight. Any other time okay, but tonight Luke didn't want even Carter Benson's company. Not even if Carter bought him drinks, as he no doubt would if allowed to. Tonight he wanted to get drunk alone so he could feel sorry for himself for what was going to happen tomorrow.

He nodded to Carter and said, "The Jabberwock with eyes of flame came whiffling through the tulgey wood," because Carter would see his lips moving but wouldn't be able to hear a word anyway, so why did it matter what he said? And nodded again before he turned back to his drink and closed his eyes. Carter wasn't a stupe; he'd get the idea and go away.

He had time to take one more sip from his drink and sigh once more, deeply, in sorrow for himself. And then the hand was on his shoulder again. Damn Carter, couldn't he take a hint?

He opened his eyes. They were blocked by something in front of them. Something pink, so it wasn't a Martian. It, whatever it was, was too close to his eyes and made them cross. So he pulled back his head to look at it.

It was a check. A very familiar type of check, although he hadn't seen one like it for a long time. A check of *Bernstein Publishers, Inc.*, his own publisher as well as Carter Benson's. Four hundred and sixteen dollars and some cents. But what the hell was Carter showing it to him for? To show off that he was still making money writing and wanted help in celebrating. To hell with him. Luke closed his eyes again.

Another and more urgent tap on his shoulder and he opened them again. The check was still there in front of them.

And he saw this time that it was made out to Luke Devereaux, and not to Carter Benson.

What the hell? He owed Bernstein money, on all those advances he'd had, not the other way around.

Just the same, he reached up with suddenly trembling fingers and took the check, held it at the proper distance from his eyes to examine it properly. It looked real all right.

He jerked back and dropped it as a Martian who was running and sliding the length of the bar as though it were an ice slide slid right through his hand and check. But Luke picked it up again without even being annoyed and turned again to Carter, who was still grinning.

"What the hell?" he asked, this time forming words exaggeratedly so Carter could read his lips.

Carter pointed to the bar and held up two fingers, then mouthed, "Want to step outside?"

It wasn't an invitation to fight, as, in happier times, that sentence had been when spoken in a bar. It had a new meaning that had developed because of the deafening din that prevailed in post-Martian drinking places. If two people wanted to talk for a minute or a few minutes without having to scream at one another or read lips, they'd step outside the front or back door onto the sidewalk or into an alley, and walk a few paces away, taking their drinks with them. If no Martian followed them or kwimmed suddenly to join them they could talk undisturbed. If a Martian did bother them they could go back inside to the maddening noise and they'd lost nothing. Bartenders understood and didn't mind people going outside with their drinks; besides, bartenders were usually too busy to notice.

Quickly Luke slid the check into his jacket and got the two drinks Carter's two fingers had signaled for and then as unobtrusively as possible led the way out the back door and into a dimly lighted alley. And luck, having hit Luke so hard and suddenly, stayed with him; no Martian followed them.

"Carter, thanks a million. And forgive me for trying to brush you off—I was just starting out on a final and solitary jag and—well, skip it. But what the hell's the check *for*?"

"Ever read a book called *Hell in Eldorado*?"

"Read it? I wrote it. But that was twelve or fifteen years ago, and it was a stinking Western."

"Exactly. Except for the *stinking*; it was a fairly good Western, Luke."

"But it's dead as a dodo. You don't mean Bernstein is reissuing it?"

"Not Bernstein, no. But Midget Books is bringing out a new pocket edition. The market in Westerns is booming and they're desperate for them. And they paid a very sweet advance guarantee to reissue your old Western."

Luke frowned. "What do you mean, Carter? Not that I want to act as though I'm looking a gift horse in the proverbial, but since when is four hundred bucks a very sweet advance on a pocket book deal? Not that it isn't a fortune to me right now, but—"

"Down, boy," Carter said. "Your share of that advance was three grand, and that's damn good for a pocket book reissue. But you owed Bernstein over two and a half grand on all those advances you've been getting, and they deducted. That check you've got there is clear and you don't owe anybody anything."

Luke whistled softly. That made it different all right.

Carter said, "Bernstein—Bernie himself—called me up last week. Mail was being returned from where you lived before and he didn't know how to reach you. I told him if he wanted to send the check care of me, I'd find you somehow. And he said—"

"How *did* you find me?"

"Found out from Margie you were in Long Beach— seems you called her some weeks ago but then never called back, and you hadn't given her an address. But I've been coming over here evenings, making the rounds of the taverns. Knew I'd run into you sooner or later."

"Miracle you did," Luke said. "My first time in one since that night I called Margie. And my last one for— I mean, it *would* have been my last time for God knows how long if you hadn't found me. But now go on about what Bernie said."

"Said to tell you to forget the science-fiction book. Science fiction's dead. Extraterrestrial stuff is just what people want to escape from right now. They've *got* Martians, in their hair. But people are still reading and there's a big swing to mystery and a bigger one to Westerns. Said to tell you that if you've actually started that science-fiction book— Have you by the way?"

"No."

"Good. Anyway, Bernie was fair about it; he said that he'd commissioned it and given you advances against it and that if you actually did have any of it done, he'd pay you a word rate for however much you've actually done—but that you can then tear it up and throw it away. He doesn't *want* it, and he wants you to stop work on it."

"Not hard when I haven't got even an idea for it. I think I had one once, in that shack of yours, but it slipped away. The night the Martians came."

"What are your plans now, Luke?"

"Tomorrow I'm going on—" Luke stopped suddenly. With a check for over four hundred dollars in his pocket he wouldn't be going on relief tomorrow after all. What *were* his plans? With the depression drop in prices he could live for months on that much money. Solvent again, he could even look up Margie. If he wanted to. Did he want to?

"I don't know," he said, and it was the answer to Carter's question and his own.

"Well, *I* know," Carter said. "I know what you're going to do if you've got any sense. You think you're burned out as a writer because you can't write science fiction any more. But you're not. You just can't write *science fiction*—and for the same reason you and everybody else doesn't want to *read* it any more. It's dead. But what's wrong with Westerns? You wrote one once—or was it only one?"

"One novel. A few short stories and novelettes. But—I don't *like* Westerns."

"Do you like digging ditches?"

"Well—not exactly."

"Look at this." Carter Benson's wallet was in his hand again and he took something from it and handed it to Luke.

It looked like another check. It *was* another check. There was barely enough light for Luke to read it. One thousand dollars, made out to Luke Devereaux, signed by W. B. Moran, Treas., Bernstein Publishers, Inc.

Carter reached across and took the check out of Luke's hand. "Not yours yet, son. Bernie sent it to me to give to you as an advance on another Western novel—if you agree to write one. He says to tell you that if you do, and if it's no worse than *Hell in Eldorado* you'll make at least five thousand out of it."

"Gimme," Luke said. He took back the check and stared at it lovingly.

His slump was over. Ideas were beginning to crowd him toward his typewriter. A lonely Western plain at dusk, a cowboy riding . . .

"Attaboy," Carter said. "Now do we hang one on to celebrate?"

"Hell, yes—or—wait a minute. Would you mind awfully if we didn't? Or at least postponed it?"

"Whatever you say. Why? Feel like diving in?"

"Exactly. I feel hot and think I should get that novel going while the mood lasts. And I'm still sober so far; this is only my fourth drink, so it's not too late. You don't mind, do you?"

"Hell, no. I understand, and I'm glad you feel that way. Nothing like the sudden turn of a new leaf." Carter put down his glass on a window sill beside him and pulled out a notebook and pencil. "Just give me your address and phone number while we're together."

Luke gave him both. Then stuck out his hand. "Thanks to hell and back. And you won't have to write to Bernie, Carter. I'll write him tomorrow—and tell him the Western's already started."

"Attaboy. And listen, Margie's been worrying about you. I could tell from the way she talked when I called her. And I had to promise I'd give her your address if I found you. Is that okay?"

"Sure, but you won't have to. I'll call her myself tomorrow." He wrung Carter's hand again and hurried off.

He felt so exhilarated and excited that it wasn't until he was on the stairs going up to his room that he discovered that he still had a half-full glass of whiskey and soda in his hand and that, fast as he'd walked, he'd carried it so carefully for ten blocks that he hadn't spilled a drop.

He laughed at himself and stopped on the landing to drink it off.

In his room he took off his suit coat and necktie and rolled up his sleeves. Put the typewriter and a stack of paper on the table and pulled up a chair. Ran paper in the typewriter. Yellow paper only. He'd already decided to do rough draft on this one so he wouldn't have to stop to look up anything. Whatever points came up that might indicate a spot of research could be taken care of on the final version.

Title? You didn't need a good title for a Western. Just so it indicated action and *sounded* like a Western. Something like *Guns Across the Border* or *Guns Across the Pecos*.

Sure, he'd settle for the *Guns Across* part except that he didn't want to write a border story again—*Hell in Eldorado* had been a border story—and he didn't know anything about the Pecos country. Better take something in Arizona; he'd traveled quite a bit around Arizona and could handle the descriptions much better.

What rivers were there in Arizona? Hmmm, the Little Colorado, but that was too long. The name, not the river. And a Trout Creek, but *Guns Across the Trout* would sound silly. *Guns Across the Date* would sound worse.

He had it. The Gila. *Guns Across the Gila*. It would even seem alliterative to people who didn't know it was pronounced Heela and not Gilla. And even if one pronounced it right it was still a plenty good title.

He centered it in caps at the top of the page.

Under it, "by Luke Devers." That was the by-line he'd used on *Hell in Eldorado* and a few other Westerns he'd written, the shorts and the novelettes. Devereaux had seemed a little fancy for the horse-opera trade. Bernie probably would want him to use it again. If he didn't, if he figured the reputation Luke had built in science fiction under his own name would carry over and help sales on a Western, that was all right too. Bernie could use either by-line he wanted to, for a thousand advance and another four thousand in eventual earnings. That was better than he'd averaged on his science-fiction novels.

A little farther down he centered "Chapter I," then spaced down a few more lines and shoved the carriage to the left. Ready to start writing.

And he was going to start right now and let the plot, or at least the details of the plot, work themselves out as he wrote.

There aren't many plots for Westerns anyway. Let's see; he could use the basic plot he'd used in one of his novelettes, *Thunder on the Range*. Two rival ranches, one run by the villain and one by the hero. And one ranch, this time, would be on each side of the Gila River and that would make the title perfect. Villain, of course, has a big ranch and hired gunmen; the hero a small ranch with maybe a few cowpokes who aren't gunmen.

And a daughter, of course. For novel length there's got to be a dame.

The plot was coming fast now.

Changing point of view. Start out with the point of view—over the shoulder—of a gunslinger hired by the villain, just coming to join up at the big ranch. But the gunslinger is a good guy at heart and is going to fall in love with the good rancher's daughter. And change sides and save the day for the right side when he finds out that—

Tried and true. A lead-pipe cinch.

Luke's fingers poised over the keyboard, hit the tab key for a paragraph indention, then started typing:

```
   As Don Marston drew nearer the fig-
ure that waited for him on the trail,
the figure resolved itself into a
grim-eyed hombre whose hands held a
stubby carbine crosswise on the pom-
mel of his saddle and . . .
```

Back and forth the typewriter's carriage, slowly at first and then faster and faster as he got into the swing of it. Forgotten in the click of keys everything but the rush of words.

And suddenly a Martian, one of the smaller ones, was sitting astride the typewriter carriage, riding it.

"Whoopie!" he yelled. *"Hi-yo, Silver! Away!* Faster, Mack, faster!"

Luke screamed.

And—

9

"Catatonia, Doctor?" the interne asked.

The ambulance physician rubbed his lantern jaw for a moment, staring down at the still figure that lay on Luke's bed.

"Very strange," he said. "Catatonic state at present, certainly, but it's probably only a phase, like the other phases." He turned to Luke's landlady, who was standing in the doorway of the room. "You say you heard a scream first?"

"That's right. An' I thought it was from *his* room and I come out in the hall to listen, but there was his typewriter banging away so I thought he was aw right and went back. An' then, two-three minutes later, glass crashed and *that* time I opened his door and went in. And there was his window busted and him laying outside it on the fire escape. Good thing for him there *was* a fire escape, throwing hisself out the window thataway."

"Strange," the doctor said.

"You're gonna take him, ain't you, doctor? Especially him bleeding like that."

"We'll take him all right. But don't worry about the bleeding. It's superficial."

"Not on my bedclothes it ain't. An' who's going to pay for that busted window?"

The doctor sighed. "That is not within my province,

Madam. But we'd better stop the bleeding from those cuts before we move him. I wonder if you would be so kind as to boil us some water?"

"Sure, Doctor."

When the landlady had left the interne glanced curiously at the doctor. "Did you really want her to boil water or—?"

"Of course not, Pete. I wanted her to boil her head, but she wouldn't have agreed to that. Always ask women to boil water if you want to get rid of them."

"It seems to work. Shall I clean up those cuts with alky here or should we take him in first?"

"Clean them up here, please, Pete. I want to look around a little. And there's a chance he might come out of it and be able to walk down those two flights under his own power."

The doctor walked over to the table on which stood a typewriter with paper in it. He started to read and stopped a moment at the by-line. "By Luke Devers," he said. "Sounds vaguely familiar, Pete. Where have I heard the name Luke Devers recently?"

"I don't know, Doc."

"Start of a Western. A novel, I'd say, since he put down *Chapter I*. Reads all right for three paragraphs—and then here's a place where a key punched right through the paper. I'd say that's how far he got when something happened to him. A Martian, no doubt."

"Is there any *other* reason why people go crazy, Doc?"

The doctor sighed. "There used to be other reasons. I guess they're not worth going crazy over, now. Well, that must have been when he screamed. And then—the landlady's right; he kept on typing for a few more lines. But come over and read them."

"In a second, Doc. This is the last cut I'm working on."

A minute later he went over to the typewriter.

"It makes sense up to there," the doctor said, pointing. "That's where a key punched through. And after that—"

"HI YO SILVER HI YO SILVER HI YO SILVER HI YO SILVER HI YO SILVER AWAY HI YO AWAY SILVER HI SILVER YO AWAY AWAY DOWN SOUTH IN THE LAND OF SILVER HI YO AWAY," the interne read.

"Sounds like a telegram the Lone Ranger might send his horse. Make anything out of it, Doc?"

"Not much. I'd guess it ties in somehow with whatever happened to him, but I can't guess how. Well, I'm new on this run, Pete. Any red tape or do we just take him in?"

"We check his wallet first."

"What for?"

"If he's got any money, any quantity of it, he'll have to go to one of the private sans. And if he's got 'in case of accident notify' identification, we notify first; maybe his relatives will foot the bill for private care and we're out from under. We're so overcrowded we have to look for an out before taking anybody."

"Is his wallet on him?"

"Yeah, hip pocket. Just a second." The interne rolled the motionless figure on the bed far enough over to take the wallet from the pocket. He brought it to the light to open it. "Three bucks," he said.

"Aren't those folded papers checks?"

"Maybe they are." The interne took them out and unfolded first one and then the other. He whistled softly. "Over fourteen hundred bucks. If they're good—"

The doctor was looking over his shoulder. "They are, unless they're forgeries. That's a reputable publishing company. Say—Luke *Devereaux* they're made out to. Luke Devers must be just a pen name, but even so it was close enough to sound familiar."

The interne shrugged. "I still haven't heard it. But then I don't read much fiction. Haven't time."

"I didn't mean it was familiar that way. But there's a girl, a nurse over at General Mental, who's been passing the word around to every doctor and psychiatrist in Long Beach to let her know if one of them gets a Luke Devereaux for a patient. He's her ex-husband, I believe. Her name is Devereaux too—I forget the first name."

"Oh. Well, then we got someone to notify all right. But how about these checks? Is he solvent or isn't he?"

"With fourteen hundred dollars?"

"But is it? They aren't endorsed. And right now he's in no shape to do any endorsing."

"Ummm," said the doctor thoughtfully. "I see what you mean. Well, as I said, I think the catatonia is a temporary phase, in his case. But if he's pronounced insane, would his endorsement be valid?"

"You·got me, Doc. But why worry about it, at least until after you've talked to this dame, his ex-wife. She must have something in mind, and maybe it's to take responsibility—and that would let us off the hook."

"Good idea. And I think I remember there's a phone right out in the hall on this floor. Hold the fort, Pete. And keep an eye on him—he could snap out of that at any time."

The doctor went out into the hall and came back five minutes later. "Well, we're in the clear all right," he said. "She's taking over. A private san—at her expense if there's any difficulty about these checks. And a private ambulance will come get him. All she asks of us is we wait ten or fifteen minutes till it gets here."

"Good deal." The interne yawned. "Wonder what made her suspect he *would* end up this way. Instable personality?"

"Partly that. But she was especially afraid something

would happen if he went back to writing—seems he
hasn't been doing or even trying any writing since the
Martians came. And she said that when he really gets
into a story and is working hard and fast on it, concen-
trating, he used to jump ten feet and fly into a violent
tizzy at even a slight interruption. When he was writing, she used to have to go around the house on tiptoe
and—well, you see what I mean."

"I guess some guys are like that, when they concentrate hard on something. Wonder what a Martian did
to him tonight?"

"Your guess is as good as mine. Whatever it was, it
happened in the heat of creation just when he was
getting started on a novel. I *would* like to know what
happened though."

"Why don't you ask me, Gentlemen?"

They whirled around. Luke Devereaux was sitting
up, on the edge of the bed. There was a Martian in
his lap.

"Huh?" said the doctor, not very brilliantly.

Luke smiled and looked at him through eyes that
were, or at least seemed, perfectly calm and sane.

He said, "I'll tell you what happened, if you're really
curious. Two months ago I went insane—I think from
pressure of trying to force myself to write when I was
in a slump and couldn't. I was in a shack on the desert
and I started hallucinating about Martians. I've been
having hallucinations ever since. Until tonight, when
I snapped out of it."

"Are you—are you *sure* they were hallucinations?"
the doctor asked. At the same time he put his hand
quietly on the interne's shoulder. As a signal, a signal
to keep quiet. If the patient, in this frame of mind,
should look down too suddenly, the trauma might happen all over again, and worse.

But the interne didn't get the signal. "Then what,"
he asked Luke, "do you call that creature in your lap?"

Luke looked down. The Martian looked up and stuck out a long yellow tongue right into Luke's face. He pulled the tongue back with a loud slurping noise. Then stuck it out again and let its tip vibrate just in front of Luke's nose.

Luke looked up and stared at the interne curiously. "There's nothing in my lap. Are you *crazy*?"

10

The case of Luke Devereaux, upon which a mono-
graph was later written by Dr. Ellicott H. Snyder (psychiatrist and proprietor of the Snyder Foundation, the
asylum for the mentally deranged to which Luke was
committed), was probably unique. At least no other
case has been authenticated by a reputable alienist in
which the patient could both see and hear perfectly
but could neither see nor hear Martians.

There were, of course, a great many people who
had the combined afflictions of blindness and deafness. Since Martians could not be felt, smelled or
tasted, these otherwise unfortunate people could have
no objective or sensory proof of their existence and
had to take the word, communicated by whatever
means, of those about them that there were such
things as Martians. And some of them never did fully
believe; one cannot blame them.

And, of course, there were millions, many millions—sane and insane, scientists, laymen and crackpots—who accepted their existence but refused to
believe that they were *Martians*.

The most numerous of these were the superstitious
and the fanatically religious who claimed that the self-
styled Martians were really banshees, brownies, dae-
mons, demons, devils, elves, fairies, fays, gnomes, gob-
lins or hobgoblins; imps, jin, kobolds, peris, pixies,

powers of darkness or powers of evil; sprites, trolls, unclean spirits or what-have-you.

All over the world, religions, sects and congregations split over this issue. The Presbyterian Church, for example, found itself split into three separate denominations. There was the Demonist Presbyterian Church, which believed they were devils out of Hell sent to punish us for our sins. There was the Scientific Presbyterian Church, which accepted that they were Martians and that the invasion of Earth by them was no more—or no less—an Act of God than are many of the earthquakes, tidal waves, fires and floods by which, from time to time, He keeps in His hand. And the Revisionist Presbyterian Church, which accepted the basic doctrine of the Demonists but took it a further step and accepted them also as Martians by simply revising their concept of the physical location of Hell. (A small splinter group of Revisionists, calling themselves the Rerevisionists, believed that, since Hell is on Mars, Heaven must be located beneath the everlasting clouds of Venus, our sister planet on the opposite side.)

Almost every other denomination found itself divided or dividing along similar—or even more startling—lines. The two outstanding exceptions were the Christian Scientists and the Roman Catholics.

The Church of Christ, Scientist, held most of its membership (and those who did wander away joined other groups rather than form a new group) by proclaiming that the invaders were neither devils nor Martians but the visible and audible product of *human error* and that if we refused to believe in their existence they would go away. A doctrine, one might note, with considerable parallel to the paranoiac delusion of Luke Devereaux, except that *his* theory worked, for him.

The Roman Catholic Church likewise maintained its integrity and a good ninety per cent of its membership due to the common sense or the Infallibility, as you prefer, of the Pope. His proclamation was to the effect that a special diet composed of Catholic theologians and Catholic scientists would be called to determine the position of the Church and that until an official announcement was made Catholics might hold opinions either way. The Diet of Cologne convened within a month and was still in session; since a condition of its adjournment was that a unanimous decision be reached, its deliberations promised to continue indefinitely and meanwhile schism was averted. True, in various countries young girls had Divine if conflicting revelations as to the nature of the Martians and their place and purpose in the universe, but none of them was recognized by the Church or gained more than local adherents. Not even the one in Chile who could show stigmata, the prints of small six-fingered hands, green, in the palms of her own hands.

Among those who inclined more to superstition than to religion, the number of theories about the Martians was as near as matters infinite. As were suggested methods of dealing with or exorcising them. (The churches at least agreed that, whatever the nature of the Martians, prayer to God to free us from them was indicated.)

But among the superstitions, books on sorcery, demonology, and black and white magic sold prodigiously. Every known form of thaumaturgy, demonomancy and conjuration was tried, and new forms were invented.

Among the soothsayers, the practitioners of astrology, numerology and the myriad other forms of prediction from the reading of cards to the study of the entrails of sheep, predicting the day and hour of the departure of the Martians became such an obsession that at no matter what hour they might have left us hundreds of the diviners must have been proved right. And any prognosticator who predicted their departure at any hour within a few days could gain followers, for a few days.

11

"The strangest case of my entire experience, Mrs. Devereaux," said Dr. Snyder.

He sat at his expensive mahogany desk in his expensively furnished office, a short, stocky man with piercing eyes in a bland moon face.

"But why, Doctor?" asked Margie Devereaux. She looked very pretty, sitting straight in a chair made for lounging. A tall girl with honey hair and blue eyes. Slender, but she filled a nurse's uniform (she had come to the sanitarium directly from her job at the hospital) beautifully in the right places. "I mean, you say you diagnose it as paranoia."

"With hysterical blindness and deafness to Martians, yes. I don't mean the *case* is complicated, Mrs. Devereaux. But he is the first and only paranoiac I have ever known who is ten times as well off, ten times as well adjusted, as though he were sane. I envy him. I hesitate to *try* to cure him."

"But—"

"Luke—I've got to know him well enough to call him by his first name—has been here a week now. He's perfectly happy—except that he keeps demanding to see you—and is working beautifully on that Western novel. Eight and ten hours a day. He has completed four chapters of it; I've read them and they are excellent. I happen to enjoy Westerns and read several

a week and I am a good judge of them. It's not hack
work; it's fine writing, up to the best of Zane Grey,
Luke Short, Haycox, the other top writers in the field.
I managed to find a copy of *Hell in Eldorado*, the one
other Western Luke wrote some years ago— Was that
before he and you were married?"

"Long before."

"—and read it. The one he's writing now is infinitely
superior. I wouldn't be surprised if it turned out to
be a best seller, or as near to a best seller as a Western
can become. Best seller or not, it should definitely
become a classic in its field. Now if I cure him of his
obsession—his purely negative obsession that there
are no Martians—"

"I see what you mean. He'd never finish it—unless
all the Martians drove him insane again."

"And happened to drive him again into exactly the
same form of aberration. A chance in thousands. Is he
going to be happier seeing and hearing Martians again
and being unable to write because of them?"

"So you suggest *not* curing him?"

"I don't know. I'm puzzled, Mrs. Devereaux—and
that's putting it mildly. It's completely unethical to
care for a patient who might be cured without attempting to cure him. I've never considered such a
thing, and I shouldn't be considering it now. Nevertheless—"

"Did you find out about those checks?"

"Yes. I telephoned his publisher, Mr. Bernstein.
The smaller of the two, the four hundred dollar one,
is money his publisher owed him. It will be all right
for us to have him endorse that and deposit, or use,
it for him in any case. At the hundred dollars a week
I charge here, it alone will cover the past week and
the next three. The—"

"But your own fee, Doctor?"

"My own fee? How can I charge a fee if I don't

even try to cure him? But about the other check, the thousand-dollar one; it was an advance against a Western novel. When I explained the circumstances to Mr. Bernstein—that Luke is definitely insane but still working well and rapidly on the novel—he was skeptical; I fear he didn't trust my literary judgment. He asked me to borrow the manuscript from Luke, telephone him back collect and read him the first chapter over the phone. I did so—the call must have cost him well over a hundred dollars—and he was enthusiastic about it. He said that if the rest of the book held up to that level, it would earn Luke at least ten thousand dollars and possibly many times that. He said that of course Luke could cash and keep the check for the advance. And that if I did anything to Luke that would stop him from finishing it, he would personally fly out here and shoot me. Not that he meant that literally, of course, and even if I thought he did I couldn't let it affect my decision, but—"

He spread his hands apologetically and a Martian appeared, sitting on one of them, said "—you, Mack," and disappeared again.

Dr. Snyder sighed. "Look at it this way, Mrs. Devereaux. Take ten thousand dollars as the minimum figure *Trail to Nowhere*—he changed the title as well as the opening from the one he originally projected—will bring Luke. The four chapters he has written in the week he's been here constitute approximately one-fourth of the book.

"On that basis, he's earned two and a half thousand dollars within the past week. If he keeps on producing at that rate, he will have earned ten thousand dollars within a month. And, even allowing for vacations between books and for the fact that he's writing unusually rapidly at present as reaction against not having been able to write at all for so long—well, he should earn at least fifty thousand dollars within the next year.

Possibly a hundred or two hundred thousand if, as Mr. Bernstein said, the book may earn 'many times' the minimum figure. Last year, Mrs. Devereaux, I cleared twenty-five thousand dollars. And *I* should cure *him*?"

Margie Devereaux smiled. "It rather frightens me to think of it myself. Luke's best year thus far, the second year of our marriage, he made twelve thousand. But one thing I don't understand, Doctor?"

"And what is that?"

"Why you sent for me. I *want* to see him, of course. But you said it would be better if I didn't, that it might disturb or distract him and cut down or even stop his production. Not that I *want* to wait any longer, but if at the rate he's writing he can finish that novel within another three weeks, might it not be wiser for me to wait that long? To make sure that, even if he—changes again, he'll at least have *that* book finished?"

Dr. Snyder smiled ruefully. He said, "I'm afraid I was given no choice, Mrs. Devereaux. Luke went on strike."

"On strike?"

"Yes, this morning he told me he wouldn't write another word unless I phoned you and asked you to come to see him. He meant it."

"Then he lost a day's writing today?"

"Oh, no. Only half an hour—it took me that long to get you on the phone. He started working again the moment I told him you'd promised to come this evening. He took my word for it."

"I'm glad. Now before I go up to see him, any instructions, Doctor?"

"Try not to argue with him, especially about his obsession. If any Martians come around, remember that he can neither see nor hear them. And that it's quite genuine; he isn't pretending in the slightest."

"And ignore them myself, of course. But you know pefectly well, Doctor, that isn't always completely possible. If, for instance, a Martian suddenly shouts in your ear when you're not expecting it—"

"Luke knows that other people still see Martians. He won't be surprised if you start suddenly. Or if you have to ask him to repeat something he just said, he'll know it's because a Martian must have been yelling louder than he was talking—that is, that *you think* a Martian is yelling."

"But if a Martian should make noise while I'm talking to him, Doctor, how is it that—even if his subconscious won't let him hear the sound the Martian makes—he can hear me clearly despite it? Or can he?"

"He can. I've checked that. His subconscious must simply tune out the Martian by pitch and he hears you clearly even though you're whispering and the Martian is screaming. It's similar to the case of people who work in boiler factories or other noisy places. Except that it's long practice rather than hysterical deafness that lets them hear and understand ordinary conversation over, or rather under, the noise level."

"I understand. Yes, I see now how he could hear despite interference. But how about *seeing*? I mean, a Martian is opaque. I don't see how even someone who doesn't believe in them can see *through* one. Suppose one got between him and me when he's looking at me. I can see how he might not see it as a Martian—as a blur, maybe—but he couldn't possibly see through it and he'd have to know *something* was there between us."

"He looks away. Common defense mechanism of specialized hysterical blindness. And his is specialized of course since he is not blind to anything but Martians.

"You see, there is a dichotomy between the conscious mind and the subconscious mind, and his subconscious mind is playing tricks on his conscious one. And it makes him turn away, or even close his eyes rather than let him find out that there's something in his direct range of vision he can't see through."

"But why does he think he turns away or closes his eyes?"

"His subconscious provides him an excuse for it, somehow. Watch and study him any time there are Martians around and you'll see how. Watch what happens any time a Martian gets in his direct range of vision."

He sighed. "I made a careful check of that the first few days he was here. I spent quite a bit of time in his room, talking with him and also in reading or pretending to read while he worked. Several times a Martian got between him and the typewriter while he was typing. Each time he'd put his hands behind his head and lean backward staring up at the ceiling—"

"He always does that when he's writing and stops to think."

"Of course. But these times his subconscious stopped his flow of thought and *made* him do it, because otherwise he'd have been looking at his typewriter and unable to see it. If he and I were talking, he'd find an excuse to get up and move if a Martian got between us. And once a Martian sat on top of his head and blocked his vision completely by letting its legs hang in front of his face. He simply closed his eyes, or I presume he did—I couldn't see through the Martian's legs either—because he remarked that his eyes were pretty tired and asked my pardon for closing them. His subconscious just wouldn't *let* him recognize that there was something there he couldn't see through."

"I'm beginning to understand, Doctor. And I suppose that if one used such an occasion to try to prove to him that there *were* Martians—told him there was one dangling its legs in front of his eyes and challenged him to open his eyes and tell you how many fingers you were holding up or something—he'd refuse to open his eyes and rationalize it somehow."

"Yes. I can see you've had experience with paranoiacs, Mrs. Devereaux. How long have you been a nurse at General Mental, if I may ask?"

"Almost six years altogether. Just ten months this time—since Luke and I separated—and for about five years before we were married."

"Would you mind telling me—as Luke's physician, of course—what caused the breakup between you?"

"I wouldn't mind at all, Doctor—but could I tell you another time? It was—a lot of little things rather than one big thing and it would take quite a while to explain it, especially if I try to be fair to both of us."

"Of course." Dr. Snyder glanced at his wristwatch. "Good Lord, I had no idea I'd kept you this long. Luke will be chewing his fingernails. But before you go up to see him, may I ask you one very personal question?"

"Of course."

"We're very shorthanded on nurses. Would you by any chance care to quit your job at General and come here to work for me?"

Margie laughed.

"What's personal about that?" she asked.

"The inducement I had in mind to get you away from them. Luke has discovered that he loves you very much and knows now he made a bad mistake in letting you get away from him. I—ah—gather from your concern that you feel the same way about him?"

"I—I'm not sure, Doctor. I feel concern, yes, and affection. And I've come to realize that at least part of the trouble between us was my fault. I'm so—so damn normal myself that I didn't sufficiently understand his psychic problems as a writer. But as to whether I can love him again—I'll want to wait until I've seen him."

"Then the inducement applies only if you decide that you do. If you decide to work and live here, the room next to his has a connecting door. Ordinarily kept locked of course, but—"

Margie smiled again. "I'll let you know before I leave, Doctor. And I guess you'll be glad to know that if I do so decide, you won't be condoning an illegality. Technically, we're still married. And I can call off the divorce at any time before it becomes final, three months from now."

"Good. You'll find him in room six on the second floor. You'll have to let yourself in; the door opens from the outside but not from the inside. When you wish to leave, just press the service buzzer and someone will come to open the door for you."

"Thanks, Doctor." Margie stood.

"And come back here, please, if you wish to talk to me on your way out. Except I hope that—ah—"

"That you won't be up that late?" Margie grinned at him and then the grin faded. "Honestly, Doctor, I don't know. It's been so long since I've seen Luke—"

She went out of the office and up thickly carpeted stairs, along the corridor until she found the door numbered six. Heard from beyond it the fast clicking of a typewriter.

Knocked gently to warn him, and then opened the door.

Luke, with his hair badly mussed but his eyes shining, jumped up from the typewriter and hurried to her, catching her just inside the door as she closed it behind her.

He said, "Margie! Oh, Margie!" and then he was kissing her. Pulling her tight against him with one arm while the other reached over her shoulder to the light switch, plunging the room into darkness.

She hadn't even had time to see if there was a Martian in the room.

Nor, she decided a few minutes later, did she care. After all, Martians weren't human.

And she was.

12

A lot of people were deciding, by that time, that Martians weren't human—when it came to letting their presence or possible presence inhibit the act of procreation.

During the first week or two after the coming of the Martians, many people began to fear that if they stayed long enough the human race might die out within a generation from lack of propagating itself.

When it became known, as it very quickly did become known, that Martians could not only see in the dark but had X-ray vision that could see through sheets, quilts, blankets, comforters and even walls, there is no denying that, for a while, the sex life of the human being—even his legitimate marital sex life—*did* take an awful beating.

Accustomed, except in the case of the degenerate and depraved, to complete privacy—except of course for his partner in the act—for even the most legal and laudable satisfaction of the flesh, people could not adjust themselves, at first, to the possibility or even probability that they were being *watched,* no matter what precautions they took. Especially since—whatever their own method of procreation—the Martians seemed to be excessively interested in, amused by and disgusted at *our* method.

The extent to which their influence proved inhibiting is reflected (at least as far as concerns legitimate marital sex relations) in the birth rate for the early months of 1965.

In January of 1965, the month that started a week more than nine months after the Coming, the birth rate in the United States dropped to 3 per cent of normal—and many of the births that did occur were early in the month and were probably due to longer-than-normal pregnancies, conception having taken place before the night of March 26, 1964. In most other countries the drop in the birth rate was almost as great; in England it was greater. Even in France the birth rate dropped to 18 per cent of normal.

In February, the tenth month (plus a week) after the Coming, the birth rate started to climb again. It was 30 per cent of normal in the United States, 22 per cent of normal in England and 49 per cent in France.

By March it was within 80 per cent of normal in all countries. And 137 per cent of normal in France; obviously the French were making up for lost time even while other countries still felt some degree of inhibition.

People were human, even if Martians weren't.

Several Kinsey-type surveys taken in April indicated that almost all married couples were again having at least occasional sex relationships. And since most of the interviews upon which these surveys were based were gleefully kibitzed by Martians who knew the facts, there is no doubt that they were much more nearly accurate in their conclusions than the original Kinsey reports of almost two decades before.

Almost universally, the sex act was practiced only at night, in complete darkness. Matins and matinees, even among newlyweds, were a thing of the past. And ear stopples were almost equally universal; even savages who had no access to drugstores selling stopples discovered the efficacy of kneaded mud for this purpose. So equipped and in complete darkness one (or, more properly, two) could ignore the presence of Martians and fail to hear their running commentaries, usually ribald.

But even under these circumstances, premarital and extra-marital sex relationships were pretty much out of the question because of the danger of being tattled on. Only the completely shameless could risk them.

And even in marriage sex relations were less frequent and, because there was always some degree of self-consciousness, not to mention the futility of whispering endearments to a stoppled ear, less enjoyable.

No, sex was not what it had been in the good old days, but at least there *was* sex, in marriage, enough of it to keep the race going.

13

The door of Dr. Snyder's office was open, but Margie Devereaux paused in the doorway until the doctor looked up and told her to come in. Then he saw that she carried two copies of a bound manuscript and his eyes brightened. "He finished?"

Margie nodded.

"And the last chapter? It's as good as the rest?"

"*I* think so, Doctor. You have time to read it now?"

"Of course. I'll take time. I was only making some notes for a paper."

"All right. If you've got paper and string, I'll get the package ready to mail while you're reading the carbon copy."

"Fine. You'll find everything you need in the cabinet there."

They were separately busied for a while. Margie finished first by a few minutes and waited till the doctor finished reading and looked up.

"It's excellent," he said. "And not only good writing, but commercially good. It will sell. And—let's see, you've been here a month now?"

"A month tomorrow."

"Then it took him only five weeks altogether. Your being here with him didn't slow him down much."

Margie smiled. "I've been careful to keep away from him during his working hours. Which hasn't been

129

too difficult, since they're my working hours too. Well, I'll take this to the post office as soon as I'm off duty."

"Don't wait; take it now. And send it airmail. Bernstein will want to rush it into print. And we'll get by without you for that long. I hope not for longer."

"What do you mean, Doctor?"

"Do you intend to stay, to keep on working for me?"

"Of course. Why shouldn't I? Isn't my work satisfactory?"

"You know perfectly well that it is. And that I want you to stay. But Margie, why should you? Your husband has earned enough in the past five weeks for the two of you to live on for at least two years. With what the Depression has done to living expenses, the two of you can live almost royally on about five thousand a year."

"But—"

"I know the money isn't all in yet, but you've got plenty to start on. Luke's fourteen hundred is safely in hand. And since your earnings here have covered my charges for Luke, whatever savings you yourself had are intact. I'll predict Bernstein will send further advances any time you ask for them, even before the book is in print."

"Are you trying to get rid of me, Doctor Snyder?"

"You know better than that, Margie. It's just that I can't see why a person should want to work when he doesn't have to. I wouldn't."

"Are you sure? While the human race, with the Martians on their necks, needs psychiatric help more than it ever has, you'd retire *now* if you happened to be able to afford to?"

Dr. Snyder sighed. "I see your point, Margie. As a matter of fact, I *could* retire, I suppose, if I sold this place. But I didn't realize a nurse would feel that way."

"This one does," Margie said. "Besides, what about Luke? I wouldn't leave here if he didn't. And do you think he should?"

Dr. Snyder's sigh was a really deep one this time. "Margie," he said, "I believe that's what's been worrying me more than anything else—except the Martians. We seem to be remarkably free of them at the moment, by the way."

"There were six of them in Luke's room when I got this manuscript."

"Doing what?"

"Dancing on him. He's lying on the bed thinking out an idea for his next book."

"Doesn't he plan to take a rest first? I wouldn't want him—" Dr. Snyder smiled wryly. "I wouldn't want him to overwork. What if he cracked up?"

"He plans to take a week off, starting tomorrow. But he says he wants to get at least a rough plot and maybe a title for his next book first. He says if he does that his subconscious will be playing around with the idea while he's resting and when he is ready to start working again it'll be easy for him to get going again."

"Which doesn't give his subconscious a rest. Or do many writers work that way?"

"I know some of them do. But I was intending to talk to you about that vacation, Doctor. After I was off duty. Shall I, now?"

"You're off duty now. And a few minutes isn't going to matter on getting that manuscript into the mail, so go ahead."

"Luke and I talked it over last night, after he told me he'd definitely finish the novel today. He says he's perfectly willing to stay here on two conditions. One, that I take off work for that week too. And the other, that the lock be taken off his door so he can have the run of the grounds. He says he'd as soon rest here as anywhere else provided he didn't feel shut in and he said we could consider it a second honeymoon if I didn't have to work either."

"Done. There's been no reason for a lock on that door anyway. I'm sometimes not certain that he's not the only sane person here, Margie. Certainly he's the best adjusted one. Not to mention the one who's earning money the fastest. Know anything at all about his next book?"

"He said he was going to place it in Taos, New Mexico, in—I think it was eighteen forty-seven. He said he'd have to do a little research on this one."

"The assassination of Governor Bent. Very interesting period. I'll be able to help him with the research. I have several books that will help him."

"Good. That may save me a trip to the library or a book store. Well—"

Margie Devereaux stood and reached for the ready-to-mail manuscript, and then paused a second and sat down again.

"Doctor," she said, "there's something else I want to talk to you about. And a few minutes won't matter on mailing this. Unless you're—"

"Go right ahead. I'm as free now as I ever am. And there's not even a Martian around."

He looked to make sure. There wasn't.

"Doctor, what does Luke really *think*? I've managed to avoid talking to him about it, but I may not always be able to. And if Martians ever *do* come up in conversation—well, I want to know how to handle it. He knows that I see and hear Martians. I can't help being startled at one once in a while. And he knows I insist on darkness and wearing ear stopples when—uh—"

"When darkness and stopped ears are indicated," Dr. Snyder prompted.

"Yes. But he knows I see and hear them and he doesn't. Does he think *I'm* insane? That everyone is crazy except Luke Devereaux? Or what?"

Dr. Snyder took off his glasses to polish them. "That's a very difficult question to answer, Margie."

"Because you don't know the answer or because it's hard to explain?"

"A little of both. The first few days Luke was here I did quite a bit of talking with him. He was a bit mixed up himself—or more than a bit, I should say. There weren't any Martians; he was sure of that. He himself had either been insane or suffering delusions while he'd been seeing them. But he couldn't account for why—if they are a mass hallucination for the rest of us—he recovered and the rest of us haven't."

"But—then he *must* think the rest of us are crazy."

"Do you believe in ghosts, Margie?"

"Of course not."

"A lot of people do—millions of people. And thousands of people have seen them, heard them, talked to them—or think they have. Now if you think you're sane, does that mean you think everyone who believes in ghosts is insane?"

"Of course not. But that's different. They're just imaginative people who *think* they've seen ghosts."

"And we're just imaginative people who think there are Martians around."

"But—but *everyone* sees Martians. Except Luke."

Dr. Snyder shrugged. "Nevertheless that's his reasoning, if you can call it that. The analogy with ghosts is his, not mine—although it's a good analogy, up to a point. Certain friends of mine, as it happens, are certain that they've seen ghosts; I don't think that means they're insane—nor that I'm insane because I haven't, or can't, or don't."

"But—you can't photograph ghosts or make recordings of their voices."

"People claim to have done both. Apparently you haven't read many books on psychic research. Not that I'm suggesting that you should—I'm just pointing out that Luke's analogy isn't completely without justification."

"Then you mean you don't think Luke is insane?"

"Of course he's insane. Either that or everyone else is insane, including you and me. And that I find impossible to believe."

Margie sighed. "I'm afraid that isn't going to help me much if he ever wants to talk about it."

"He may never want to. He talked to me rather reluctantly, I'm afraid. If he does, let him do the talking and just listen. Don't try to argue with him. Or, for that matter, to humor him. But if he starts changing in any way or acting different, let me know."

"All right. But why? If you're not trying to cure him, I mean."

"Why?" Dr. Snyder frowned. "My dear Margie, your husband is insane. Right now it is a very advantageous form of insanity—he's probably the luckiest man on Earth—but what if the form of his insanity should change?"

"*Can* paranoia change to another form?"

Dr. Snyder made an apologetic gesture. "I keep forgetting that I don't have to talk to you as a layman. What I should have said is that his systematized delusion might change to another and less happy one."

"Like believing again in Martians, but not believing in human beings?"

Dr. Snyder smiled. "Hardly so complete a switch as that, my dear. But it's quite possible—" His smile vanished. "—that he might come to believe in neither."

"You're surely joking."

"No, I'm not. It's really quite a common form of paranoia. And, for that matter, a form of belief held by a great many sane people. Haven't you heard of solipsism?"

"The word sounds familiar."

"Latin, from *solus* meaning alone and *ipse* meaning self. Self alone. The philosophical belief that the self is the only existent thing. Logical result of starting reasoning with 'Cogito, ergo sum'—I think, therefore I am—and finding oneself unable to accept any secondary step as logical. The belief that the world around you and all the people in it, except yourself, are simply something you imagine."

Margie smiled. "I remember now. It came up in a class in college. And I remember wondering, why not?"

"Most people wonder that at some time or other, even if not very seriously. It's such a tempting thing to believe, and it's so completely impossible to disprove. For a paranoiac, though, it's a ready-made delusion that doesn't even have to be systematized or even rationalized. And since Luke already disbelieves in Martians, it's only another step."

"You think it's a possibility that he might take that step?"

"Anything's a possibility, my dear. But all we can do is to watch carefully and be prepared for any impending change by getting some intimation of it in advance. And you're the one best situated for getting an advance warning."

"I understand, Doctor. I'll watch carefully. And thank you, for everything."

Margie stood again. This time she picked up the package and went out with it.

Dr. Snyder watched her go and then sat for a while staring at the doorway through which she had disappeared. He sighed more deeply than before.

Damn Devereaux, he thought. Impervious to Martians and married to a girl like that.

No one man should be so lucky; it wasn't fair.

His own wife— But he didn't want to think about his own wife.

Not after he'd just been looking at Margie Devereaux.

He picked up his pencil and pulled back in front of him the pad on which he had been making notes for the paper he intended to present that evening at the meeting of his cell of the P.F.A.M.

14

Yes, there was the P.F.A.M. The Psychological Front Against Martians. Going strong if still—in mid-July now, almost four months after the Coming—apparently going nowhere.

Almost every psychologist and psychiatrist in the United States. In every country in the world almost every psychologist and psychiatrist belonged to an equivalent organization. All of these organizations reported their findings and theories (there were, unfortunately, more theories than findings) to a special branch of the United Nations which had quickly been set up for the purpose and which was called the O.C.P.E.—Office for the Coordination of Psychological Effort—the main job of which was to translate and distribute reports.

The Translation Department alone filled three large office buildings and provided employment for thousands of multilingual people. If nothing else.

Membership in the P.F.A.M. and in the similar organizations in other countries was voluntary and unpaid. But almost everyone qualified belonged and the lack of pay didn't matter since every psychologist and psychiatrist who could remain sane himself was earning plenty.

There were, of course, no conventions; large groups of psychologists were as impractical as large groups for any other purpose. Large groups of people meant large groups of Martians and the sheer volume of interference made speaking impractical. Most P.F.A.M. members worked alone and reported by correspondence, received reams of reports of others and tried out on their patients whatever ideas seemed worth trying.

Perhaps there was progress of a sort. Fewer people were going insane, at any rate. This may or may not have been, as some claimed, that most people insufficiently stable to stand up to the Martians had already found escape from reality in insanity.

Others credited the increasingly sensible advice that the psychologists were able to give to those still sane. Incidence of insanity had dropped, they claimed, when it was fully realized that it was safe, mentally, to ignore Martians only up to a point. You had to swear back at them and lose your temper at them once in a while. Otherwise the pressure of irritation built up in you as steam builds up pressure in a boiler without a safety valve, and pretty soon you blew your top.

And the equivalently sensible advice not to try to make friends with them. People did try, at first, and the highest percentage of mental casualties is believed to have been among this group. A great many people, men and women of good will, tried that first night; some of them kept on trying for quite a while. A few—saints they must have been, and wonderfully stable people to boot—never did quit trying.

The thing that made it impossible was that the Martians moved *around* so. No single Martian ever stayed long in one place or in contact with one person, one family or one group. It just might have been possible, unlikely as it seems, for an extremely patient human being to have achieved friendly footing with a Martian, to have gained a Martian's confidence, if that human being had had the opportunity of protracted contact with a given Martian.

But no Martian was *given*, in that sense. The next moment, the next hour—at most the next day—the man of good will would find himself starting from scratch with a different Martian. In fact, people who tried to be nice to them found themselves changing Martians oftener than those who swore back at them. Nice people bored them. Conflict was their element; they loved it.

But we digressed from the P.F.A.M.

Other members preferred to work in small groups, cells. Especially those who, as members of the Psychological Front, were studying, or attempting to study, the psychology of the Martians. It is an advantage, up to a point, to have Martians around when one is studying or discussing them.

It was to such a cell, a group of six members, that Dr. Ellicott H. Snyder belonged, and it was due to meet that evening. And now he was pulling paper into the roller of his typewriter; the notes for the paper are finished. He wishes he could simply talk from the notes themselves; he likes to talk and detests writing. But there is always the possibility that Martian interference will make coherent talking impossible at a cell meeting and necessitate papers being passed around to be read. Even more important, if the cell members approve the content of a paper it is passed up to a higher echelon and given wider consideration, possibly publication. And this particular paper should definitely merit publication.

15

Dr. Snyder's paper began:

It is my belief, that the Martians'
one psychological weakness, their
Achilles' heel, is the fact that
they are congenitally unable to lie.
I am aware that this point has been
stated and disputed, and I am aware
that many—and particularly our Russian colleagues—firmly believe that
the Martians can and do lie, that
their reason for telling the truth
about our own affairs, for never
once having been caught in a prov-
able lie about terrestrial matters,
is twofold. First, because it makes
their tattling more effective and
more harassing, since we cannot
doubt what they tell us. Second, because by never being provably untrue
in small things, they prepare us to
believe without doubt whatever Big
Lie about their nature and their purpose here they are telling us. The
thought that there must be a Big Lie
is one that would seem more natural

to our Russian friends than to most
people. Having lived for so long
with their own Big Lie . . .

Dr. Snyder stopped typing, reread the start of his
last sentence and then went back and x'd it out. Since,
he hoped, this particular paper would be distributed
internationally, why prejudice some of his readers in
advance against what he was going to say.

I believe, however, that it can be
clearly proved through a single logical argument that the Martians not
only do not lie but cannot.
It is obviously their purpose to ha-
rass us as much as possible.
Yet they have never made the one
claim, the one statement, that would
increase our misery completely past
bearing; they have never once told
us *that they intend to stay here permanently.* Since Coming Night, their
only answer, when they deign to answer at all, to the question, however worded, of when they intend to
go home or how long they intend to
stay is that it is ''none of our business'' or words to that effect.
For most of us the only thing that
makes survival desirable is *hope,*
hope that someday, whether tomorrow
or ten years from now, the Martians
will leave and we'll never see them
again. The very fact that their coming was so sudden and unexpected
makes it seem quite possible that
they'll leave the same way.

If the Martians could lie, it is impossible to believe that they would not tell us that they intend to be permanent residents here. Therefore, they cannot lie.

And a very welcome corollary of this simple step in logic is that it becomes immediately obvious that they know their stay here is *not* permanent. If it were, they would not have to lie in order to increase our unhap—

A high-pitched chuckle sounded only an inch or two from Dr. Snyder's right ear. He jumped a few inches, but very carefully didn't turn, knowing it would put the Martian's face unbearably close to his own.

"*Ver-y* clever, Mack, *ver-y* clever. And screwy as a bedbug, screwy as a bedbug."

"It's perfectly logical," said Dr. Snyder. "It's absolutely proved. You can't lie."

"But I can," said the Martian. "Work on the logic of that a while, Mack."

Dr. Snyder worked on the logic of that, and groaned. If a Martian said he could lie, then either he was telling the truth and he could lie, or else he was lying and—

There was a sudden shrieking laugh in his ear.

And then silence in which Dr. Snyder took the paper from his typewriter, manfully resisted the impulse to fold it so he could tear it into paper dolls, and tore it into small pieces instead. He dropped them into the wastebasket and then dropped his head in his hands.

"Dr. Snyder, are you all right?" Margie's voice.

"Yes, Margie." He looked up and tried to compose his face; he must have succeeded for apparently she saw nothing wrong. "My eyes were tired," he explained. "I was just resting them for a moment."

"Oh. Well, I mailed the manuscript. And it's still only four o'clock. Are you sure there's nothing you want me to do before I take off."

"No. Wait, yes. You might look up George and tell him to change the lock on Luke's door. Put on an ordinary one, I mean."

"All right. Finish your paper?"

"Yes," he said. "I finished my paper."

"Good. I'll find George." She went away and he heard the click of her heels on the stairs leading down toward the janitor's quarters in the basement.

He stood, almost without effort. He felt terribly tired, terribly discouraged, terribly futile. He needed a rest, a nap. If he slept, and overslept to miss dinner or the cell meeting, it wouldn't matter. He needed sleep more than he needed food or pointless argument with fellow psychiatrists.

He trudged wearily up the carpeted stairs to the second floor, started along the corridor.

Paused outside Luke's door and found himself glaring at it. The lucky bastard, he thought. In there thinking or reading. And, if there were Martians around, not even knowing it. Not able to see them or hear them.

Perfectly happy, perfectly adjusted. Who was crazy, Luke or everybody else?

And having Margie, too.

Damn him. He should throw him to the wolves, to the other psychiatrists, and let them experiment with him, probably make him as miserable as anybody else by curing him—or making him insane in some other and not so fortunate direction.

He should, but he wouldn't.

He went on to his own room, the one he used here when he didn't want to go home to Signal Hill, and shut the door. Picked up the telephone and called his wife.

"I don't think I'll be home tonight, dear," he said. "Thought I'd better tell you before you started dinner."

"Something wrong, Ellicott?"

"Just that I'm terribly tired. Going to take a nap and if I sleep through—well, I need the sleep."

"You have a meeting tonight."

"I may miss that, too. If I do go to it, though, I'll come home afterwards instead of back here."

"Very well, Ellicott. The Martians have been unusually bad here today. Do you know what two of them—"

"Please, dear. I don't want to hear about Martians. Tell me some other time, please. Good-bye, dear."

Putting down the phone, he found himself staring into a haunted face in the mirror, his own face. Yes, he needed sleep, badly. He picked up the phone again and called the receptionist, who also worked the switchboard and kept records. "Doris? I'm not to be disturbed under any circumstances. And if there are any callers, tell them I'm out."

"All right, Doctor. For how long?"

"Until I call back. And if that isn't before you go off duty and Estelle comes on, explain to her, will you? Thanks."

He saw his face in the mirror again. Saw that his eyes looked hollow and that there was at least twice as much gray in his hair as had been there four months ago.

So Martians can't lie, huh? he asked himself silently.

And then let him carry the thought to its horrible conclusion. If Martians could lie—and they could— then the fact that they did not claim they were staying here permanently wasn't proof that they weren't.

Perhaps they got more sadistic pleasure out of letting us hope so they could keep on enjoying our sufferings than by ending humanity by denying it hope. If everyone committed suicide or went insane, there'd be no sport for them; there'd be no one left to torment.

And the logic of that paper had been so simply beautiful and so beautifully simple . . .

His mind felt fogged now and for a moment he couldn't remember where the flaw in it had been. Oh, yes. If someone says he can lie, he can; otherwise he'd be lying in saying he could lie, and if he is already lying—

He pulled his mind out of the circle before it made him dizzier. He took off his coat and tie and hung them over the back of a chair, sat down on the edge of the bed and took off his shoes.

Lay back on the bed and closed his eyes.

Suddenly, a moment later, jumped almost three feet off the bed as two raucous and almost unbelievably loud Bronx cheers went off simultaneously, one in each ear. He'd forgotten his ear stopples.

He got up and put them in, lay down again. This time he slept.

And dreamed.

About Martians.

16

The scientific front against the Martians wasn't organized as was the psychological front, but it was even more active. Unlike the psych boys, who had their hands full with patients and could spare only stolen time for research and experimentation, the physical scientists were putting in full time and overtime studying the Martians.

Research in every other direction was at a standstill.

The active front was every big laboratory in the world. Brookhaven, Los Alamos, Harwich, Braunschweig, Sumigrad, Troitsk and Tokuyama, to mention only a few.

Not to mention the attic, cellar or garage of every citizen who had a smattering of knowledge in any field of science or pseudoscience. Electricity, electronics, chemistry, white and black magic, alchemy, dowsing, biotics, optics, sonics and supersonics, typology, toxicology and topology were used as means of study or means of attack.

The Martians *had* to have a weakness somewhere. There just *had* to be *something* that could make a Martian say "Ouch."

They were bombarded with alpha rays, with beta, gamma, delta, zeta, eta, theta and omega rays.

They were, when opportunity offered (and they nei-

ther avoided nor sought being experimented on),
caught in multi-million-volt flashes of electricity, subjected to strong and weak magnetic fields and to mi-
crowaves and macrowaves.

They were subjected to cold near absolute zero and
to heat as hot as we could get it, which is the heat of
nuclear fission. No, the latter was not achieved in a
laboratory. An H-bomb test that had been scheduled
for April was, after some deliberation by authorities,
ordered to proceed as planned despite the Martians.
They knew all our secrets by then anyway so there
was nothing to lose. And it was hoped that a Martian
might be inspecting the H-bomb at close range when
it was fired. One of them was sitting on it. After the
explosion he kwimmed to the bridge of the admiral's
flagship, looking disgusted. "Is *that* the best you can
do for firecrackers, Mack?" he demanded.

They were photographed, for study, with every kind
of light anybody could think of: infrared, ultraviolet,
fluorescent, sodium, carbon arc, candlelight, phospho-
rescence, sunlight, moonlight and starlight.

They were sprayed with every known liquid, including prussic acid, heavy water, holy water and Flit.

Sounds they made, vocal or otherwise, were recorded by every known type of recording device. They
were studied with microscopes, telescopes, spectro-
scopes and iconoscopes.

Practical results, zero; nothing any scientist did to
any Martian made him even momentarily uncomfortable.

Theoretical results, negligible. Very little was
learned about them that hadn't been known within a
day or two of their arrival.

They reflected light rays only of wave lengths within
the visible spectrum (.0004 mm. to .00076 mm.). Any
radiation above or below this band passed through
them without being affected or deflected. They could
not be detected by X-rays, radio waves or radar.

They had no effect whatsoever on gravitational or magnetic fields. They were equally unaffected by every form of energy and every form of liquid, solid or gaseous matter we could try on them.

They neither absorbed nor reflected sound, but they could create sound. That perhaps was more puzzling to scientists than the fact that they reflected light rays. Sound is simpler than light, or at least is better understood. It is the vibration of a medium, usually air. And if the Martians weren't *there* in the sense of being real and tangible, how could they cause the vibration of air which we hear as sound? But they did cause it, and not as a subjective effect in the mind of the hearer for the sound could be recorded and reproduced. Just as the light waves they reflected could be recorded and studied on a photographic plate.

Of course no scientist, by definition, believed them to be devils or demons. But a great many scientists refused to believe that they came from Mars—or, for that matter, anywhere else in our universe. Obviously they were a different kind of matter—if matter at all, as we understand the nature of matter—and must come from some other universe where the laws of nature were completely different. Possibly from another dimension.

Or, still more likely, some thought, they themselves had fewer or more dimensions than we.

Could they not be two-dimensional beings whose appearance of having a third dimension was an illusory effect of their existence in a three-dimensional universe? Shadow figures on a movie screen appear to be three-dimensional until you try to grab one by the arm.

Or perhaps they were projections into a three-dimensional universe of four- or five-dimensional beings whose intangibility was due somehow to their having *more* dimensions than we could see and understand.

17

Luke Devereaux awoke, stretched and yawned, feeling blissful and relaxed on this, the third morning of the week's vacation he was taking after having finished *Trail to Nowhere*. The best-earned vacation he'd ever had, after finishing a book in five weeks flat. A book that would probably make him more money than any book he'd written to date.

No worries about his next book, either. He had the main points of the plot well in mind already and if it weren't for Margie being so insistent that he take a vacation he'd probably be a chapter or so into it already. His fingers itched to get at the typewriter again.

Well, he'd made the bargain that he'd take a vacation only if Margie did too, and that made it a second honeymoon, practically, and just about perfect.

Just about perfect? he asked himself. And found his mind suddenly shying away from the question. If it wasn't perfect, he didn't *want* to know why it wasn't.

But why didn't he want to know? That was one step further removed from the question itself, but even so it was vaguely troubling.

I'm thinking, he thought. And he shouldn't be thinking, because thinking might spoil everything somehow. Maybe that was why he'd worked so hard at writing, to keep from thinking?

But to keep from thinking what? His mind shied again.

And then he was out of the half-sleep and was awake, and it came back to him.

The Martians.

Face the fact you've been trying to duck, the fact that everybody else still sees them and you don't. That you're insane—and you know you aren't—or that everybody else is.

Neither makes sense and yet one or the other must be true and ever since you saw your last Martian over five weeks ago you've been ducking the issue and trying to avoid thinking about it—because thinking about such a horrible paradox might drive you nuts again like you were before and you'd start seeing—

Fearfully he opened his eyes and looked around the room. No Martians. Of course not; there *weren't* any Martians. He didn't know how he could be so utterly, completely certain of that fact, but he *was* utterly and completely certain.

Just as certain as he was that he was sane, now.

He turned to look at Margie. She still slept peacefully, her face as innocent as a child's, her honey hair spread about on the pillow beautiful even in disarray. The sheet had slipped down to expose the tender pink nipple of a softly rounded breast and Luke raised himself on one elbow and then leaned across to kiss it. But very gently so as not to waken her; the faint light coming in at the window told him it was still quite early, not much after dawn. And also so as not to wake himself, *that* way, because the last month had taught him that she'd have nothing to do with him that way by daylight, only at night and wearing those damned things in her ears so he couldn't talk to her. The damn Martians. Well, that part of it wasn't too bad; this was a second honeymoon, not a first, and he was thirty-seven and not too ambitious early in the morning.

He lay back and closed his eyes again, but already he knew he wasn't going back to sleep.

And he didn't. Maybe it was ten minutes later, maybe twenty, but he found himself getting wider awake every second, so he slid cautiously out of bed and into his clothes. It was still not quite half past six, but he could go out and take a walk around the grounds until it was late enough. And Margie might as well get as much sleep as she could.

He picked up his shoes and tiptoed out into the hall with them, closing the door quietly behind him and sitting down on the top step of the stairway to put on his shoes.

None of the outer doors of the sanitarium was ever locked; patients who were confined at all—fewer than half of them—were confined to private rooms except while under supervision. Luke let himself out the side door.

Outdoors was clear and bright, but almost too cool. Even in early August a dawn can be almost cold in Southern California; this one was, and Luke shivered a bit and wished he'd put on a pullover sweater under his sport jacket. But the sun was fairly well up and it wouldn't stay that cool long. If he walked fairly briskly he'd be all right.

He walked fairly briskly over to the fence and then along parallel to it. The fence was redwood and six feet high. There was no wire atop it and any reasonably agile person, Luke included, could have climbed it; the fence was for privacy rather than for a barrier.

For a moment he was tempted to climb it and walk in freedom for half an hour or so, and then decided against it. If he was seen, either going over or coming back, Dr. Snyder might worry about it and curtail his privileges. Dr. Snyder was very much of a worrier. Besides, the grounds were quite large; he could do plenty of walking right inside them.

He kept walking, along the inside of the fence. To the first corner, and turned.

And saw that he wasn't alone, wasn't the only early
riser that morning. A small man with a large black
spade beard was sitting on one of the green benches
that were scattered around the grounds. He wore gold-
rimmed glasses and was meticulously dressed down to
highly polished black shoes topped by light gray spats.
Luke looked curiously at the spats; he hadn't known
anyone wore them any more. The spade-bearded one
was looking curiously up over Luke's shoulder.

"Beautiful morning," Luke said. Since he'd already
stopped, it would have been rude not to speak.

The bearded man didn't answer. Luke turned and
looked over his own shoulder, found himself looking
up into a tree. But he saw nothing there that one
does not usually see looking up into a tree, leaves and
branches. Not a bird's nest, not even a bird.

Luke turned back and the bearded man still stared
up into the tree, still hadn't looked at Luke. Was the
man deaf? Or—?

"I beg your pardon," Luke said. An awful suspicion
came over him when there wasn't any answer to that.
He stepped forward and touched the man lightly on
the shoulder. The shoulder twitched slightly. The
bearded man reached up a hand and rubbed it casu-
ally, but without turning his gaze.

What would he do if I hauled off and slugged him?
Luke wondered. But instead he reached out a hand
and moved it back and forth in front of the man's
eyes. The man blinked, and then took off his glasses,
rubbed first one eye and then the other, put the
glasses back on and stared again into the tree.

Luke shivered, and walked on.

My God, he thought; he can't see me, can't hear
me, doesn't believe I'm here. Just as *I* don't believe—

But, damn it, when I touched him he felt it, only—

Hysterical blindness, Doc Snyder explained it to
me, when I asked him why, if Martians were *there*, I

didn't see blank spots that I couldn't see through, even if I couldn't see *them*.

And he explained that I—

Just like that man—

There was another bench and Luke sat down on it, turned to stare back at the bearded one, still sitting on his own bench twenty yards back. Still sitting there, still looking up in the tree.

At something that isn't there? Luke wondered.

Or at something that isn't there for me but is there for him, and which of us is right?

And he thinks that *I* don't exist and I think I do, and which of us is right about that?

Well, *I* am, on that point if no other. I think, therefore I am.

But how do I know *he's* there?

Why couldn't *he* be a figment of *my* imagination?

Silly solipsism, the type of wondering just about everybody goes through sometime during adolescence, and then recovers from.

But it gives to wonder all over again when you and other people start seeing things differently or start seeing different things.

Not Spade-Beard; he was just another nut. No significance there. Just that maybe, just maybe, that little encounter with him had put Luke's mind to working on what could be the right track.

The night he'd got drunk with Gresham and just before he'd passed out there'd been that Martian, the one he'd cussed back at. "I *'nvented* you," he remembered telling the Martian.

Well?

What if he really had? What if his mind, in drunkenness, had recognized something his sober mind hadn't known?

What if solipsism *wasn't* silly?

What if the universe and everything and everybody

in it were simply figments of the imagination of Luke Devereaux?

What if I, Luke Devereaux, *did* invent the Martians that evening they came, when he was in Carter Benson's shack on the desert near Indio?

Luke got up and started walking again, faster, to speed up his mind. He thought back, hard, about that evening. Just before the knock had come on the door he'd had the start of an idea for a science-fiction novel he'd been trying to write. He'd been thinking, "What if the Martians . . ."

But he couldn't remember what the rest of that thought had been. The Martian's knock had interrupted it.

Or had it?

What if, even though his conscious mind had not formulated the thought clearly it had already worked itself out in his subconscious mind: *What if the Martians are little green men, visible, audible, but not tangible, and what if, a second from now, one of them knocks on that door and says, "Hi, Mack. Is this Earth?"*

And went on from there.

Why not?

Well, for one reason, he'd worked out other plots—hundreds of them if you counted short stories—and none of them had happened the instant he'd thought of them.

But—what if, that night, something in the conditions had been a little different? Or, and this seemed more likely, there'd been a slip in his brain—from brain fatigue and from worry over his slump—and the part of his mind which separated "fact," the fictional universe which his mind ordinarily projected about him, from "fiction," the stuff he conceived and wrote *as* fiction and which would in that case really be fiction-within-fiction?

It made sense, however nonsensical it sounded.

But what had happened, then, a little over five weeks ago, when he'd quit believing in Martians? Why did other people—if other people were themselves products of his, Luke's, imagination—keep on believing in and seeing something Luke himself no longer believed in, and which therefore no longer existed?

He found another bench and sat down on it. That was a tough one to figure out.

Or was it? His mind had received a shock that night. He couldn't remember what it was except that it concerned a Martian, but from what it had done to him— knocked him temporarily into a catatonic state—it must have been a severe shock all right.

And just maybe it had knocked belief in Martians out of his conscious mind, the mind that was thinking right now, without having cleared from his subconscious the error between fact and fiction—between the projected "real" universe and the plot for a story— which had brought the fictional Martians into seemingly real existence in the first place.

He wasn't paranoiac at all. Simply schizophrenic.

Part of his mind—the conscious, thinking part— didn't believe in Martians, knew, in fact, that they didn't exist.

But the deeper part, the subconscious that was the creator and sustainer of illusions, hadn't got the message. *It* still accepted the Martians as real, as real as anything else, and so, of course, did those other beings of his imagination and its, human beings.

In excitement, he got up and started to walk again, rapidly this time.

That made it easy. All he had to do was get the message to his subconscious mind.

It made him feel silly to do it, but he subvocalized:

Hey, there aren't any Martians. Other people shouldn't be seeing them either.

Had that done it? Why not, if he had the right overall answer and he was sure he had.

He found himself at a far corner of the grounds and turned to head back toward the kitchen. Breakfast should be ready by now and he should be able to tell by the actions of other people whether they still saw and heard Martians.

He glanced at his watch and saw that it was ten after seven, still twenty minutes before the first call for breakfast, but there was a table and chairs in the big kitchen and from seven o'clock on early risers were welcome to have coffee there ahead of the regular breakfast.

He let himself in the back door and looked around. The cook was busy at the stove; an attendant was readying a tray for one of the confined patients. The two nurses' aides who doubled as waitresses on the breakfast shift weren't around; they were probably setting tables in the dining room.

Two patients were having coffee at the table, both elderly women, one in a bathrobe and the other in a housecoat.

All looked calm and peaceful, no sign of a disturbance. Not that he'd see the Martian end of one if one did happen, but he should be able to tell by the reactions of the people he *could* see. He'd just have to watch for indirect evidence.

He poured himself a cup of coffee and took it to the table, sat down in a chair. Said, "Good morning, Mrs. Murcheson," to the one of the two women he knew; Margie had happened to introduce them yesterday.

"Good morning, Mr. Devereaux," Mrs. Murcheson said. "And your beautiful wife? Still sleeping?"

"Yes. I got up early for a walk. Beautiful morning."

"It seems to be. This is Mrs. Randall, Mr. Devereaux, if you two don't know each other."

Luke murmured politely.

"Pleased, I'm sure, Mr. Devereaux," said the other elderly lady. "If you've been out on the grounds perhaps you could tell me where my husband is, so I won't have to look *all* over for him?"

"I saw only one other person," Luke said. "A man with a spade beard?"

She nodded and Luke said, "Right near the northwest corner. Sitting on one of the benches, staring up into a tree."

Mrs. Randall sighed. "Probably thinking out his big speech. He thinks he's Ishurti this week, poor man." She pushed back her chair. "I'll go and tell him coffee is ready."

Luke started to push back his own chair and opened his mouth to say that he'd go for her. Then he remembered that Spade-Beard could neither see nor hear him, so the carrying of a message would be embarrassingly ineffective. He refrained from offering.

When the door had closed, Mrs. Murcheson laid a hand on his arm. "Such a *nice* couple," she said. "It's too bad."

"She seems nice," Luke said. "I—uh—didn't get to meet him. Are they both—uh—?"

"Yes, of course. But each thinks that only the other is. Each thinks he is here just to stay with and take care of the other." She leaned closer. "But I have my suspicions, Mr. Devereaux. I think they're both spies, just pretending to be insane. *Venusian spies!*" Both s's hissed and Luke leaned back and under pretext of wiping coffee from his lips managed to wipe the spittle from his cheek as well.

To change the uncomfortable subject he asked, "What did she mean by saying he thought he was shirty this week?"

"Not shirty, Mr. Devereaux. Ishurti."

The word or name sounded familiar to him, now that he'd heard it repeated, but he couldn't place it.

But he realized suddenly that it might be embarrassing if Mrs. Randall brought her husband to the table while he was there, so instead of asking more questions he finished his coffee quickly and excused himself, saying he wanted to go upstairs to see if his wife was awake for breakfast yet.

He made his escape just in time; the Randalls were coming in the back way.

Outside their room he heard Margie moving around inside, knocked lightly so as not to startle her, and then went in.

"Luke!" She threw her arms around him and kissed him. "Have a walk around the grounds?" She was partly dressed—bra, panties and shoes, and the dress she'd dropped onto the bed to free her hands would complete the ensemble.

"That and one cup of coffee. Put that dress on and we'll be just in time for breakfast."

He dropped into a chair and watched as she lifted the dress overhead and started the usual series of contortions, ungraceful but fascinating to watch, that women always go through in pulling a dress over their heads.

"Margie, who or what is Ishurti?"

There was a muffled sound from inside the dress and then Margie's head came out of the collar of it, staring at him a bit incredulously as she smoothed the dress down her body. "Luke, haven't you been reading the newspa— That's right, you haven't been. But from back when you were reading them, you ought to remember Yato Ishurti!"

"Oh, sure," Luke said. The two names together reminded him now who the man was. "Has he been much in the news lately?"

"Much in the news? He's *been* the news, Luke, for the past three days. He's to make a speech tomorrow on the radio, to the whole world; they want *everybody* to listen in and the newspapers have been giving it top headlines ever since the announcement."

"A radio speech? But I thought that Martians were supposed to—I mean, I thought Martians interrupted them."

"They can't any more, Luke. That's *one* thing we've finally licked them on. Radio has developed a new type of throat mike, one that the Martians can't cut in on. That was the big story about a week ago, before Ishurti's announcement."

"How does it work? The mike, I mean."

"It doesn't pick up sound at all, as such. I'm no technician so I don't know the details, but it picks up just the vibrations of the speaker's larynx direct and translates them into radio waves. He doesn't even have to speak out loud; he just— What's the word?"

"Subvocalizes," Luke said, remembering his experiment in trying to talk to his subconscious that way, only minutes ago. Had it worked? He'd seen no indication of a Martian around. "But what's the speech *about*?"

"Nobody knows, but everyone assumes it's about Martians, because what else, right now, would he want to talk to the whole world about? There are rumors— nobody knows whether they're true or not—that one of them has finally made a sensible contact with him, propositioned him by telling him on what terms the Martians will leave. And it seems possible, doesn't it? They must have a leader, whether it's a king or a dictator or a president or whatever else they might call him. And if he made contact, isn't Ishurti the man he'd go to?"

Luke managed not to smile, even to nod noncom-

mittally. What a letdown Ishurti was going to have. By
tomorrow . . .

"Margie, when did you last see a Martian?"

She looked at him a bit strangely. "Why, Luke?"

"I—just wondered."

"If you must know, there are two of them in the
room right now."

"Oh," he said.

It hadn't worked.

"I'm ready," Margie said. "Shall we go down?"

Breakfast was being served. Luke ate moodily, not
tasting the ham and eggs at all; they might as well
have been sawdust. *Why* hadn't it worked?

Damn his subconscious; couldn't it hear him
subvocalize?

Or didn't it believe him?

He knew suddenly that he'd have to get away,
somewhere. Here, and he might as well face it that
here was an insane asylum even if one called it a sanitarium, here was no place to work out a problem like
that.

And wonderful as Margie's presence was, it was a
distraction.

He'd been alone when he'd invented the Martians;
he'd have to be alone again to exorcise them. Alone
and away from everything and everybody.

Carter Benson's shack near Indio? Of course; *that's
where it had all started!*

Of course it was August now and it would be hellish
hot out there by day, but for that very reason he could
be sure that Carter himself wouldn't be using it. So
he wouldn't have to ask Carter's permission and not
even Carter would know that he was there and be
able to give him away if there was a search for hin.
Margie didn't know about the place; he'd never happened to mention it to her.

But he'd have to plan carefully. Too early to make

his getaway now because the bank didn't open until nine and that would have to be his first stop. Thank God Margie had opened their account as a joint account and had brought out a signature card for him to sign. He'd have to cash a check for several hundred so he'd have enough to buy a used car; there wasn't any other way of getting out to Benson's shack. And he'd sold his own car before he'd left Hollywood.

Got only two hundred and fifty dollars for it, too, although a few months before—while there was still such a thing as pleasure driving—it would have brought him five hundred. Well, that meant he'd be able to buy one cheaply now; for less than a hundred he'd be able to pick up something good enough to get him there and let him run into Indio for shopping— if what he had to do took him that long.

"Anything wrong, Luke?"

"Nup," he said. "Not a thing." And realized he might as well start preparing the groundwork for his escape. "Except that I'm a little dopey. Couldn't sleep last night; doubt if I got more than a couple hours solid sleep all night."

"Maybe you should go up to the room and take a nap now, darling."

Luke pretended to hesitate. "Well—maybe later. If I get actually sleepy. Right now I feel sort of dull and logy but I doubt if I could sleep."

"Okay. Anything special you'd like to do?"

"How about a few games of badminton? That just might tire me out enough so I *could* sleep a few hours."

It was a little windy for badminton, but they played for half an hour—that made it half-past eight—and then Luke yawned and said that now he really *was* sleepy. "Maybe you'd better come up with me," he suggested. "If you want to get anything from the room, you can, and then you won't have to bother me until time for lunch, if I sleep that long."

"You go ahead; there's nothing I'll want. I promise not to bother you till twelve."

He kissed her briefly, wishing it could be a longer kiss since he might not see her again for a while, and went into the building and up to the room.

He sat down at the typewriter first and wrote a note to her, telling her he loved her but that there was something important he had to do, and not to worry because he'd be back soon.

Then he found Margie's purse and took enough money to pay cab fare into town in case he could catch a cab. It would save time if he could, but even if he had to walk all the way to the bank he could be there by eleven and that would be in plenty of time.

Then he looked out of the window to see if he could find Margie on the grounds, and couldn't. Tried the window at the end of the hall and couldn't see her from there either. But when he went quietly downstairs he heard her voice coming from the open doorway of Dr. Snyder's office. ". . . not really worried," he heard her saying, "but he did act just a bit strange. I don't think, though, that he . . ."

He let himself quietly out of the side door and strolled to the back corner of the grounds where a grove of trees hid the fence from the buildings.

His only danger now was that someone outside the fence might see him climb it, and phone the police or the sanitarium.

But no one did.

18

It was the fifth day of August, 1964. A few minutes
before 1 P.M. in New York City. Other time zones,
other times, all over the world. This was to be the big
moment, maybe.

Yato Ishurti, Secretary-General of the United Nations, sat alone in a small studio at Radio City. Ready
and waiting.

Hopeful and frightened.

The throat mike was in place. There were stopples
in his ears to prevent aural distraction once he had
started to speak. And he would close his eyes, too,
the instant the man behind the control room window
nodded to indicate that he was on the air, so he could
not be subject to visual distraction either.

Remembering that the mike was not yet activated,
he cleared his throat as he watched the little glass
window and the man behind it.

He was about to speak to the largest audience that
had ever listened to the voice of one man, ever, anywhere. Barring a few savages and children too young
to talk or to understand, just about every human being
on Earth would listen to him—either directly or through
the voice of a translator.

Hurried as they had been, preparations had been
exhaustive. Every government on Earth had cooper-
ated fully, and every active radio station in the world

163

would pick up and rebroadcast what he had to say. Every active radio station and many that had been abandoned but quickly reactivated for the purpose. And all the ships at sea.

He must remember to speak slowly and to pause at the end of each sentence or few sentences so the thousands of translators who would relay the broadcasts in non-English-speaking countries could keep up with him.

Even tribesmen in the most primitive countries would hear; arrangements had been made wherever possible to have natives come in and listen to on-the-spot translations at the nearest receiving sets. In civilized countries every factory and office not already closed by the Depression would be closed down while employees gather around radios and P.A. systems; people staying home who had no radios were requested to join neighbors who had.

As near as matters, three billion people would be hearing him. And, as near as matters, one billion Martians.

If he succeeded he would become the most famous— But Ishurti pulled his mind quickly away from that selfish thought. He must think of humanity, not of himself. And if he succeeded he must retire at once, not try to capitalize on success.

If he failed— But he must not think about that either.

No Martian seemed to be present in the studio, none in the part of the control room he could see through the little window.

He cleared his throat again, and just in time. He saw the man beyond the control room window flick a switch and then nod to him.

Yato Ishurti closed his eyes, and spoke.

He said: "People of the world, I speak to you and through you to our visitors from Mars. Mostly I speak to them. But it is necessary that you listen too, so that when I have spoken you can answer a question that I shall ask you."

He said: "Martians, you have not, for whatever reason of your own, taken us into your confidence as to why you are here among us.

"Possibly you are truly vicious and evil and our pain gives you pleasure.

"Possibly your psychology, your pattern of thinking, is so alien to ours that we could not understand even if you tried to explain to us.

"But I do not believe either of these things."

He said: "If you really are what you seem or pretend to be, quarrelsome and vindictive, we would find you, at least on rare occasion, arguing or fighting among yourselves.

"This we have never seen or heard.

"Martians, you are putting on an act, pretending to be something that you are not."

Across Earth, there was a stir as people moved.

Ishurti said: "Martians, you have an ulterior purpose in doing what you have been doing. Unless your reason is beyond my power to comprehend, unless your purpose is beyond the scope of human logic, it can and must be one of only two things.

"It can be that your purpose is good; that you came here for *our* good. You knew that we were divided, hating one another, warring and ever on the verge of final war. It can be that you reasoned that, being what we are, we could be united only by being given a common cause, and a common hatred that transcends our hatreds of one another and makes them now seem so ridiculous that they are difficult for us to remember.

"Or it is possible that your purpose is less benevolent, but still not inimical. It is possible that, learning we stand—or stood—on the verge of space travel, you do not want us on Mars.

"It could be that, on Mars, you are corporeal and vulnerable and that you are afraid of us; you fear that we might try to conquer you, either soon or centuries from now. Or perhaps we merely bore you—certainly our radio programs must have—and you simply do not want our company on your planet."

He said: "If either of those basic reasons is the real one, and I believe that one or the other of them is, you knew that merely *telling* us to behave ourselves or to stay away from Mars would antagonize us rather than accomplish your purpose.

"You wanted us to see for ourselves and to *volunteer* to do as you wish.

"Is it important that we know or guess correctly which of these two basic purposes is your true one?

"Whichever it is, I will prove to you that you have accomplished it."

He said: "I speak, and I shall now prove that I speak, for all the peoples of Earth."

He said: "We pledge that we are through fighting among ourselves.

"We pledge that we shall not, we shall never, send a single spaceship to your planet—unless someday you invite us to, and I think that we might need persuading, even then."

He said solemnly: "And now the proof. *People of Earth*, are you with me in both of those pledges? If you are, prove it now, wherever you are, with an affirmative in your loudest voice! But so that the translators may have caught up with me, please wait until I give the signal by saying . . .

" . . . Now!"

"YES!

"SI!

"OUI!

"DAH!

"HAY!

"JA!
"SIM!
"JES!
"NAM!
"SHI!
"LAH!"

And thousands of other words that all mean the same thing, simultaneously from the throat and from the heart of every human being who had been listening.

Not a *no* or a *nyet* among them.

It was the damnedest sound ever made. Compared to it an H-bomb would have been the dropping of a pin, the eruption of Krakatao would have been the faintest of whispers.

There could be no doubt that every Martian on Earth must have heard it. Had there been an atmosphere between the planets to carry sound, the Martians on *Mars* would have heard it.

Through ear stopples and inside a closed soundproofed broadcasting studio, Yato Ishurti heard it. And felt the building vibrate with it.

He spoke no further word to anticlimax that magnificent sound. He opened his eyes and nodded to the man in the control room to take him off the air. Sighed deeply after he had seen the switch move and reached up and took the stopples from his ears.

Stood, spent emotionally, walked slowly and let himself into the little anteroom between the studio and the hallway, paused there a moment to regain his composure.

Turned by chance and saw himself in a mirror on the wall.

Saw the Martian seated cross-legged atop his head, caught its eye in the mirror, and its grin, heard it tell him, "——you, Mack."

Knew that he must do what he had come prepared to do in case of failure.

Took from his pocket the ceremonial knife and removed it from its sheath.

Sat himself upon the floor in the manner required by tradition. Spoke briefly to his ancestors, performed the brief preliminary ritual, and then with the knife—

Resigned as secretary-general of the United Nations.

19

The stock market had closed at noon the day of Ishurti's speech.

It closed at noon again on August 6th, the following
day, but for a different reason; it closed for an indefi-
nite period as a result of an emergency order issued
by the President. Stocks that morning had opened at
a fraction of their previous day prices (which were a
fraction of their pre-Martian prices), were finding no
takers and declining rapidly. The emergency order
stopped trading while at least some stocks were still
worth the paper they were printed on.

In an even more sweeping emergency measure that
afternoon, the government decided upon and announced a ninety per cent reduction in the armed
forces. In a press conference, the President admitted
the desperation behind this decision; it would greatly
swell the ranks of the unemployed, nevertheless the
measure was necessary as the government was for all
practical purposes bankrupt and it was cheaper to
maintain men on relief than in uniform. And all other
nations were making similar cuts.

And similarly, despite all cuts, tottering upon the
verge of bankruptcy. Almost any of the established
orders would have been a pushover for a revolution—
except for the fact that not even the most fanatical of
revolutionaries *wanted* to take over under such
circumstances.

Harassed, heckled, hounded, helpless, hamstrung, harried and harrowed, the average citizen of the average country looked with heartfelt horror to a hideous future and hankered hungrily for a return to the good old days when his only worries were death, taxes and the hydrogen bomb.

PART THREE

THE GOING
OF THE MARTIANS

1

IN AUGUST of the year 1964 a man with the mildly improbable name of Hiram Pedro Oberdorffer, of Chicago, Illinois, invented a contraption which he called an anti-extraterrestrial subatomic supervibrator.

Mr. Oberdorffer had been educated in Heidelberg, Wisconsin. His formal education had ended at the eighth grade, but in the fifty-odd years that followed he had become an inveterate reader of popular science magazines and of science articles in Sunday supplements and elsewhere. He was an ardent theorist and, in his own words (and who are we to gainsay them), he "knew more science than most of them laboratory guys."

He was employed, and had been for many years, as janitor of an apartment building on Dearborn Street near Grand Avenue, and lived in a basement apartment of two rooms in the same building. In one of the two rooms he cooked, ate and slept. In the other

173

room he lived the part of his life that mattered; it was his workroom.

Besides a work bench and some power tools the workroom contained several cabinets, and in and on the cabinets and piled on the floor or in boxes were old automobile parts, old radio parts, old sewing machine parts and old vacuum cleaner parts. Not to mention parts from washing machines, typewriters, bicycles, lawn mowers, outboard motors, television sets, clocks, telephones, tinkertoys, electric motors, cameras, phonographs, electric fans, shotguns and Geiger counters. Infinite treasures in a little room.

His janitorial duties, especially in summer, were not too onerous; they left him ample time for inventing and for his only other pleasure which was, in good weather, to sit and relax and think in Bughouse Square, which was only a ten-minute walk from where he lived and worked.

Bughouse Square is a city park one block square and it has another name but no one ever uses the other name. It is inhabited largely by bums, winos and crackpots. Let us have it clearly understood, however, that Mr. Oberdorffer was none of these. He worked for a living and he drank only beer and that in moderate quantity. Against accusations of being a crackpot, he could have *proved* that he was sane. He had papers to show it, given him upon his release from a mental institution where once, some years before, he had been briefly incarcerated.

Martians bothered Mr. Oberdorffer much less than they bothered most people; he had the very excellent good fortune to be completely deaf.

Oh, they bothered him some. Although he couldn't listen, he loved to talk. You might even say that he thought out loud, since he habitually talked to himself all the while he was inventing. In which case, of course, Martian interference was no nuisance; although he couldn't hear his own voice he knew perfectly well what he was saying to himself whether or not he was being drowned out. But he had one friend besides himself to whom he liked to talk, a man named Pete, and he found that Martians did interfere occasionally in his one-sided conversations with Pete.

Every summer Pete lived in Bughouse Square, whenever possible on the fourth bench to the left along the walk that diagonalled from the inner square toward the southeast corner. In the fall Pete always disappeared; Mr. Oberdorffer assumed, not too incorrectly, that he flew south with the birds. But the following spring Pete would be there again and Mr. Oberdorffer would take up the conversation again.

It was a very one-sided conversation indeed, for Pete was a mute. But he loved to listen to Mr. Oberdorffer, believing him to be a great thinker and a great scientist, a view with which Mr. Oberdorffer himself was in complete accord, and a few simple signals sufficed for his end of the conversation—a nod or shake of the head to indicate yes or no, a raising of the eyebrows to request further explanation or elucidation. But even these signals were rarely necessary; a look of admiration and rapt attention usually sufficed. Even more rarely was recourse to the pencil and pad of paper which Mr. Oberdorffer always carried with him necessary.

Increasingly, though, this particular summer Pete had been using a new signal—cupping a hand behind his ear. It had puzzled Mr. Oberdorffer the first time Pete had used this signal, for he knew that he was talking as loudly as ever, so he had passed the pad and pencil to Pete with a request for explanation, and Pete had written: "Cant here. Marsheys too noysy."

So Mr. Oberdorffer had obliged by talking more loudly, but it annoyed him somewhat to have to do so. (Not as much, however, as his talking so loudly—

even after the interference had ceased, since he had
no way of knowing when the Martians stopped heckling—annoyed the occupants of adjacent benches.)

Even when, this particular summer, Pete did not
signal for an increase in volume, the conversations
were no longer quite as satisfactory as they had once
been. All too frequently the expression on Pete's face
showed all too clearly that he was listening to something else instead of or in addition to what Mr. Oberdorffer was telling him. And whenever at such times
Mr. Oberdorffer looked about he'd see a Martian or
Martians and know that he was being heckled, to
Pete's distraction and therefore indirectly to his own.

Mr. Oberdorffer began to toy with the idea of doing
something about the Martians.

But it wasn't until in mid-August that he definitely
decided to do something about them. In mid-August
Pete suddenly disappeared from Bughouse Square.
For several days running, Mr. Oberdorffer failed to
find him there and he started to ask the occupants of
other benches—those whom he had seen often enough
to recognize as regulars—what had happened to Pete.
For a while he got nothing but head shakes or other
obvious disclaimers such as shrugs; then a man with
a gray beard started to explain something to him so
Mr. Oberdorffer said that he was deaf and handed
over the pad and pencil. A temporary difficulty arose
when the bearded one turned out to be unable to read
or write, but between them they found an intermedi-
ary who was barely sober enough to listen to gray
beard's story and put it in writing for Mr. Oberdorffer
to read. Pete was in jail.

Mr. Oberdorffer hastened to the precinct station
and after some difficulty due to the fact that there are
many Petes and he didn't know his best friend's last
name finally learned where Pete was being held and
hurried to see him to help if he could.

It turned out that Pete had already been tried and convicted and was past help for thirty days, although he gladly accepted a loan of ten dollars to enable him to buy cigarettes for that period.

However he managed to talk to Pete briefly and to learn, via the pad and pencil route, what had happened.

Shorn of misspellings, Pete's story was that he had done nothing at all, the police had framed him; besides, he'd been a little drunk or he'd never have tried to shoplift razor blades from a dime store in broad daylight with Martians around. The Martians had enticed him into the store and had promised to act as lookout for him and then had ratted on him and called copper the moment he had his pockets full. It was all the fault of the Martians.

This pathetic story so irked Mr. Oberdorffer that, as of that very moment, he decided definitely to *do* something about the Martians. That very evening. He was a patient man but he had reached the limit of his patience.

Enroute home, he decided to break a long standing habit and eat at a restaurant. If he didn't have to interrupt his thinking to cook a meal for himself, he'd be off to a quicker start.

In the restaurant he ordered pigs' knuckles and sauerkraut and, while waiting for it to be brought to him, he started his thinking. But very quietly so as not to disturb other people along the counter.

He marshaled before him everything he'd read about Martians in the popular science magazines, and everything he'd read about electricity, about electronics and about relativity.

The logical answer came to him at the same time as the pigs' knuckles and sauerkraut. "It's got," he told the waitress, "to be an anti-extraterrestrial subatomic supervibrator! That's the only thing that will get them." Her answer, if any, went unheard and is unrecorded.

He had to stop thinking while he ate, of course, but he thought loudly the rest of the way home. Once in his own place, he disconnected the signal (which was a flashing red light in lieu of a bell) so no tenant of the building could interrupt him to report a leaking faucet or a recalcitrant refrigerator, and then he started to build an anti-extraterrestrial subatomic supervibrator.

"We use this outboard motor for power," he thought, suiting action to word. "Only the propeller it comes off and gives a generator to make the D.C. at—how many volts?" And when he figured that out, he stepped up the voltage with a transformer and then stepped it sidewise into a spark coil, and went on from there.

Only once did he encounter a serious difficulty. That was when he realized that he would need a vibrating membrane about eight inches in diameter. There was nothing in his workroom that would serve the purpose and since it was then eight o'clock and all stores were closed he almost gave up for the evening.

But the Salvation Army saved him, when he remembered it. He went out and over to Clark Street, walked up and down until a Salvation Army lassie came along to make the rounds of the taverns. He had to get as high as an offer of thirty dollars to the cause before she would agree to part with her tambourine; it is well she succumbed at that figure for it was all the money he had with him. Besides, if she had not agreed he would have been strongly tempted to grab the tambourine and run with it, and that would in all probability have landed him in jail with Pete. He was a portly man, a slow runner, and short of wind.

But the tambourine, with the jangles removed, turned out to be exactly right for his purpose. Covered with a light sprinkling of magnetized iron filings and

placed between the cathode tube and the aluminum
saucepan which served as a grid, it would not only
filter out the unwanted delta rays but the vibration of
the filings (once the outboard motor was started)
would provide the required fluctuation in the
inductance.

Finally, a full hour after his usual bedtime, Mr. Oberdorffer soldered the last connection and stepped
back to look at his masterpiece. He sighed with satisfaction. It was good. It should work.

He made sure that the airshaft window was open
as high as it would raise. The subatomic vibrations had
to have a way out or they would work only inside the
room. But once free they would bounce back from
the heaviside layer and, like radio waves, travel all
around the world in seconds.

He made sure there was gasoline in the tank of the
outboard motor, wound the cord around the spinner,
prepared to pull the cord—and then hesitated. There'd
been Martians in the room off and on all evening but
there was none present now. And he'd rather wait till
one was present again before starting the machine, so
he could tell right away whether or not it worked.

He went into the other room and got a bottle of
beer from the refrigerator and opened it. Took it back
with him into the workroom and sat sipping it and
waiting.

Somewhere outside a clock struck, but Mr. Oberdorffer, being deaf, did not hear it.

There was a Martian, sitting right atop the antiextra-
terrestrial subatomic supervibrator itself.

Mr. Oberdorffer put down his beer, reached over
and pulled the cord. The motor spun and caught, the
machine ran.

Nothing happened to the Martian.

"Take it a few minutes to build up potential," Mr.

Oberdorffer explained, to himself rather than to the Martian.

He sat down again, picked up his beer. Sipped it and watched and waited for the few minutes to pass.

It was approximately five minutes after eleven o'clock, Chicago time, on the evening of August 19th, a Wednesday.

2

On the afternoon of August 19, 1964, in Long Beach,
California, at four o'clock in the afternoon (which
would have been six o'clock in the afternoon in Chicago, just about the time Mr. Oberdorffer reached
home full of pigs' knuckles and sauerkraut, ready to
start work on his anti-extraterrestrial et cetera), Margie
Devereaux looked around the corner of the doorway
into Dr. Snyder's office and asked, "Busy, Doctor?"

"Not at all, Margie. Come in," said Dr. Snyder, who
was swamped with work. "Sit down."

She sat down. "Doctor," she said, a bit breathlessly.
"I've an idea finally as to how we can find Luke."

"I certainly hope it's a good one, Margie. It's been
two weeks now."

It had been a day longer than that. It had been
fifteen days and four hours since Margie had gone up
to their room to waken Luke from his nap and had
found a note waiting for her instead of a husband.

She'd run with the note to Dr. Snyder and their
first thought, since Luke had had no cash except a few
dollars that had been in Margie's purse, had been the
bank. But a call to the bank had brought them the
information that he had drawn five hundred dollars
from the joint account.

Only one further fact had come to light subsequently. Police, the following day, had learned that

less than an hour after Luke's call at the bank a man answering his description but giving a different name had bought a used car from a lot and paid one hundred dollars cash for it.

Dr. Snyder was not without influence at the police department and the entire Southwest had been circularized with descriptions of Luke and of the car, which was an old 1957 Mercury, painted yellow. Dr. Snyder himself had similarly circularized all mental institutions in the area.

"We agreed," Margie was saying, "that the place he'd most likely go to would be that shack on the desert where he was the night the Martians came. You still think so?"

"Of course. He thinks he *invented* the Martians—says so in that note he left for you. So what's more natural than that he'd go back to the same place, try to reconstruct the same circumstances, to undo what he thinks he did. But I thought you said you didn't have the faintest idea where the shack is."

"I still haven't except that it's within driving distance of L.A. But I just remembered something, Doctor, I remember Luke telling me, several years ago, that Carter Benson had bought a shack somewhere—near Indio, I think. That could be the one. I'll bet it is."

"But you called this Benson, didn't you?"

"I called him, yes. But all I asked him was whether he'd seen or heard from Luke since Luke left here. And he said he hadn't but promised to let me know if he did hear anything. But I didn't ask him if Luke had used his shack last March! And he wouldn't have thought to volunteer the information, because I didn't tell him the whole story or that we thought Luke might be going back to wherever he was last March. Because—well, it just never occurred to me."

"Hmmm," said Dr. Snyder. "Well, it's a possibility.

But would Luke use the shack without Benson's permission?"

"He probably had permission last March. This time he's hiding out, don't forget. He wouldn't want even Carter to know where he went. And he'd know Carter wouldn't be using it himself—not in August."

"Quite true. You want to phone Benson again, then? There's the phone."

"I'll use the one in the outer office, Doctor. It might take a while to reach him, and you *are* busy, even if you say you aren't."

But it didn't take long to reach Carter Benson after all. Margie was back within minutes, and her face was shining.

"Doctor, it *was* Carter's place Luke used last March. And I've got instructions how to get there!" She waved a slip of paper.

"Good girl! What do you think we should do? Phone the Indio police or—?"

"Police nothing. I'm going to him. As soon as I'm through with my shift."

"You needn't wait for that, my dear. But are you sure you should go alone? We don't know how much his illness has changed and progressed, and you might find him—disturbed."

"If he isn't I'll disturb him. Seriously, Doctor, don't worry. I can handle him, no matter what." She glanced at her wristwatch. "A quarter after four. If you really don't mind my leaving now, I can be there by nine or ten o'clock."

"You're sure you don't want to take one of the attendants with you?"

"Very sure."

"All right, my dear. Drive carefully."

3

On the evening of the third day of the third moon of
the season of kudus (at, as near as matters, the same
moment Mr. Oberdorffer, in Chicago, was making in-
quiries in Bughouse Square about his missing friend)
a witch doctor named Bugassi, of the Moparobi tribe
in equatorial Africa, was called before the chief of his
tribe. The chief's name was M'Carthi, but he was no
relative of a former United States senator of the same
name.

"Make juju against Martians," M'Carthi ordered
Bugassi.

Of course he did not really call them *Martians*. He
used the word *gnajamkata*, the derivation of which is:
gna, meaning "Pygmy," plus *jam*, meaning "green,"
plus *kat*, meaning "sky." The final vowel indicates a
plural, and the whole translates as "green Pygmies
from the sky."

Bugassi bowed. "Make big juju," he said.

It had damned well better be a big juju, Bugassi
knew.

The position of a witch doctor among the Moparobi
is a precarious one. Unless he is a very good witch
doctor indeed, his life expectancy is short. It would
be even shorter were it not quite rare for the chief to
make an official demand upon one of his witch doctors, for tribal law decreed that one of them who failed

184

must make a contribution of meat to the tribal larder. And the Moparobi are cannibals.

There had been six witch doctors among the Moparobi when the Martians came; now Bugassi was the last survivor. One moon apart (for taboo forbids the chief to order the making of a juju less than a full moon of twenty-eight days after the making of the last previous juju) the other five witch doctors had tried and failed and made their contributions.

Now it was the turn of Bugassi and from the hungry way M'Carthi and the rest of the tribe stared at him it appeared they would be almost as satisfied if he failed as if he succeeded. The Moparobi had not tasted meat for twenty-eight days and they were meat hungry.

All of Africa was meat hungry.

Some of the tribes, those who had lived exclusively or almost exclusively from hunting, were actually starving. Other tribes had been forced to migrate vast distances to areas where vegetable foods, such as fruits and berries, were available.

Hunting was simply no longer possible.

Almost all of the creatures man hunts for food are fleeter of foot or of wing than he. They must be approached upwind and by stealth until he is within killing distance.

With Martians around there was no longer any possibility of stealth. They loved to help the natives hunt. Their method of helping was to run—or to kwim— well ahead of the hunter, awakening and alerting his quarry with gladsome cries.

Which made the quarry scamper like hell.

And which made the hunter return empty-handed from the hunt, ninety-nine times out of a hundred without having had the opportunity to shoot an arrow or throw a spear, let alone having hit something with either one.

It was a Depression. Different in type but at least as punishing in effect as the more civilized types of Depression that were rampant in the more civilized countries.

The cattle-herding tribes were affected too. The Martians loved to jump onto the backs of cattle and stampede them. Of course, since a Martian had no substance or weight, a cow couldn't *feel* a Martian on its back, when the Martian leaned forward and screamed "Iwrigo 'm N'gari" ("Hi-yo, Silver") in Masai at the top of his voice in the cow's ear while a dozen or more other Martians were screaming "Iwrigo 'm N'gari" into the ears of a dozen or more other cows and bulls, the stampede was on.

Africa just didn't seem to *like* the Martians.

But, back to Bugassi.

"Make big juju," he had told M'Carthi. And a big juju it was going to be, literally and figuratively. When, shortly after the green Pygmies had come from the sky, M'Carthi had called in his six witch doctors and had conferred long and seriously with them. He had tried his best to persuade or to order them to pool their knowledge so that one of them, using the knowledge of all six, could make the greatest juju that had ever been made.

They had refused and even threats of torture and death could not move them. Their secrets were sacred and more important to them than their lives.

But a compromise had been reached. They were to draw lots for their turns, a moon apart. And each agreed that if, and only if, he failed, he would confide all of his secrets, including and in particular the ingredients and incantations that went into his juju, before he made his contribution to the tribal stomach.

Bugassi had drawn the longest twig and now, five moons later, he had the combined knowledge of all of the others as well as his own—and the witch doctors of the Moparobi are famed as the greatest of all Africa. Furthermore, he had exact knowledge of every thing and every word that had gone into the making of the five jujus that had failed.

With this storehouse of knowledge at his fingertips, he had been planning his own juju for a full moon now, ever since Nariboto, the fifth of the witch doctors, had gone the way of all edible flesh. (Of which Bugassi's share, by request, had been the liver, of which he had saved a small piece; well putrefied by now, it was in prime condition to be included in his own juju.)

Bugassi knew that his own juju could not fail, not only because the results to his own person were unthinkable if it did fail, but because—well, the combined knowledge of *all* of the witch doctors of the Moparobi simply *could* not fail.

It was to be a juju to end all jujus, as well as all Martians.

It was to be a monster juju; it was to include every ingredient and every spell that had been used in the other five and in addition was to include eleven ingredients and nineteen spells (seven of which were dance steps) which had been his own very special secrets, completely unknown to the other five.

All the ingredients were at hand and when assembled, tiny as most of them were individually, they would fill the bladder of a bull elephant, which was to be their container. (The elephant, of course, had been killed six months before; no big game had been killed since the Martians came.)

But the assembling of the juju would take all night, since each ingredient must be added with its own spell or dance and other spells and dances interspersed with the adding of ingredients.

Throughout the night no Moparobi slept. Seated in a respectful circle around the big fire, which the women replenished from time to time, they watched while Bugassi labored, danced and cast spells. It was a strenuous performance; he lost weight, they noticed sadly.

Just before dawn, Bugassi fell supine before M'Carthi, the chief.

"Juju done," he said from the ground.

"Gnajamkata still here," said M'Carthi grimly. They were very much still there; they had been very active all night, watching the preparations and joyfully pretending to help them; several times they had made Bugassi stumble in his dancing and once fall flat on his face by darting unexpectedly between his legs while he had danced. But each time he had patiently repeated the sequence so no step would be lost.

Bugassi raised himself on one elbow in the dirt. With the other arm he pointed to the nearest large tree.

"Juju must hang clear of ground," he said.

M'Carthi gave an order, and three black bucks leaped to obey it. They tied a rope of woven vines around the juju and one of them shinned up the tree and passed the rope over a limb; the other two hoisted the juju and when it was ten feet off the ground Bugassi, who had meanwhile climbed painfully to his feet, called to them that it was high enough. They secured it there. The one in the tree came down and they rejoined the others.

Bugassi went over to the tree, walking as though his feet hurt (which they did) and stood under the juju. He faced the east, where the sky was gray now and the sun just under the horizon, and folded his arms.

"When sun strike juju," he said solemnly if a bit hoarsely, "gnajamkata go."

The red rim of the sun came into sight over the horizon; its first rays struck the top of the tree in which the juju hung, moved downward.

In a very few minutes now, the first rays of the sun would reach the juju.

By coincidence or otherwise it was the exact moment when, in Chicago, Illinois, United States of America, one Hiram Pedro Oberdorffer, janitor and inventor, sat sipping beer and waiting for his anti-extraterrestrial subatomic supervibrator to build up potential.

4

And as near as matters to three quarters of an hour before that exact moment, at about 9:15 P.M. Pacific Time in a shack on the desert near Indio, California, Luke Devereaux was making his third drink of the evening.

It was his fourteenth thwarting evening at the shack.

It was the fifteenth evening since his escape, if one can call so simple a walk-away an escape, from the sanitarium. The first evening had been thwarting too, but for a different reason. His car, the old '57 Mercury he had bought for a hundred dollars, had broken down in Riverside, about half-way between Long Beach and Indio. He'd had it towed to a garage, where they'd told him it couldn't possibly be fixed until the next afternoon. He'd spent a dull evening and a bad night (it seemed so strange and so lonesome to be sleeping alone again) at a Riverside hotel.

He'd spent the following morning shopping and carrying his purchases to the garage to load them in the car while a mechanic was working on it. He'd bought a used portable typewriter, of course, and some stationery. (He'd been in the process of choosing the typewriter when, at 10 A.M. Pacific Time, Yato Ishurti's speech had come on the air, and business had been suspended while the proprietor turned on a radio and everyone in the store had gathered around it. Knowing Ishurti's fundamental premise—that there really *were* Martians—to be completely wrong, Luke had been mildly annoyed at the interruption to his shopping, but had found himself quite amused at Ishurti's ridiculous reasoning.)

He bought a suitcase and some extra clothing, razor, soap and comb, and enough food and liquor so he wouldn't have to make a shopping trip into Indio for at least a few days after he got to the shack. He hoped what he had to accomplish there wouldn't take any longer than that.

He got his car back—with a repair bill almost half as much as the original cost of it—in midafternoon and reached his destination just before dark. He found himself too tired to try very hard that evening, and, anyway, he realized that he had forgotten something: Alone, he had no way of telling whether or not he had succeeded.

The next morning he drove back to Indio and bought himself the best and most expensive table model radio he could find, a set that would bring in programs from all over the country, a set on which he could find newscasts emanating from somewhere or other almost any time of day or evening.

Any newscast would tell him.

The only trouble was that for two weeks, until tonight, the newscasts had consistently told him wrong. They'd told him that the Martians were still around. Not that the newscasts opened with the statement, "The Martians are still with us," but almost every story concerned them at least indirectly or concerned the Depression and the other troubles they were causing.

And Luke was trying everything he could think of, and almost going crazy trying.

He *knew* the Martians were imaginary, the product (like everything else) of his own imagination, that he had invented them that evening five months ago, in March, when he'd been trying to plot a science-fiction novel. He'd *invented* them.

But he'd invented hundreds of other plots and none of them had really happened (or *seemed* really to happen) so there had been something different that evening, and he was trying everything to reconstruct the exact circumstances, the exact frame of mind, the exact everything.

Including, of course, the exact amount of drinking, the exact tinge of inebriety, since that might have been a factor. As he had done while he was here the period preceding that evening, he stayed strictly sober by day—no matter how badly hung over he might awaken—pacing the floor and getting desperate (then, for a plot; now, for an answer). Now, as then, he would let himself start drinking only after he'd made and fed himself a dinner and then he'd space his drinks and pace his drinking very carefully—at least until he'd given up in disgust for the evening.

What was wrong?

He'd invented Martians by imagining them, hadn't he? Why couldn't he *un*-invent them now that he'd ceased to imagine them, now that he'd learned the truth? He had, of course, as far as he himself was concerned. Why wouldn't other people stop seeing and hearing them?

It must be a psychic block, he told himself. But naming it didn't help.

He took a sip of his drink and stared at it. Trying, for the thousandth time since he'd been here, to remember *exactly* how many drinks he'd had that night in March. It wasn't many, he knew; he hadn't been feeling them, any more than he was feeling the two he'd already had tonight before this one.

Or didn't the drinking have anything to do with it after all?

He took a second sip of his drink, put it down and started pacing. *There aren't any Martians*, he thought. *There never were any; they existed—like everything and everybody else—only while I imagined them. And I no longer imagine them.*

Therefore—

Maybe that had done it. He went over to the radio and turned it on, waited for it to warm up. Listened to several discouraging items, realizing that even if he had just succeeded, it would be at least minutes, since Martians weren't seen everywhere all the time, before anyone began to realize that they were gone. Until the newscaster happened to say, "At this very moment, right here in the studio, a Martian is trying to . . ."

Luke flicked off the radio and swore.

Took another sip of his drink and paced some more.

Sat down and finished his drink and made another one.

Had a sudden idea.

Maybe he could outwit that psychic block by going around it instead of through it. The block could only be because, even though he knew he was right, he lacked sufficient faith in himself. Maybe he should imagine something else, something completely different, and when his imagination brought it into being, even his damned subconscious couldn't deny it, and then in that moment of undeniability—

It was worth trying. There was nothing to lose.

But he'd imagine something that he really *wanted*,

and what did he want—outside of getting rid of Martians—most right at this moment?

Margie, of course.

He was lonesome as hell after these two weeks of solitude. And if he could imagine Margie here, and by imagining bring her here, he *knew* he could break that psychic block. With one arm tied behind his back, or with both arms around Margie.

Let's see, he thought: *I'll imagine that she's driving here in her car, already through Indio and only half a mile away. Pretty soon I'll hear the car.*

Pretty soon he heard the car.

He made himself walk, not run, to the door and open it. He could see headlights coming. Should he—now—?

No, he'd wait till he was *sure.* Not even when the car came close enough that he thought he could recognize it as Margie's; a lot of cars look alike. He'd wait until the car had stopped and Margie got out of it and he *knew.* And then, in that golden moment, he'd think *There Aren't Any Martians.*

And there wouldn't be.

In a few minutes, the car would be here.

It was approximately five minutes after nine o'clock (P.M.), Pacific Time. In Chicago it was five minutes after eleven and Mr. Oberdorffer sipped beer and waited for his supervibrator to build up potential; in equatorial Africa it was dawn and a witch doctor named Bugassi stood with crossed arms under the greatest juju ever made, waiting for the sun's first rays to strike it.

Four minutes later, one hundred and forty-six days and fifty minutes after they appeared, the Martians disappeared. Simultaneously, from everywhere. Everywhere on Earth, that is.

Wherever they went, there is no authenticated instance of one having been seen since that moment.

Seeing Martians in nightmares and in delirium tremens is still common, but such sightings can hardly be called authenticated.

To this day . . .

To this day

POSTLOGUE

To this day, nobody knows why they came or why they left.

Not that a great many people do not *think* they know, or at least have very strong opinions on the subject.

Millions of people still believe, as they believed then, that they were not Martians but devils and that they went back to hell and not back to Mars. Because a God who sent them to punish us for our sins became again a merciful God as a result of our prayers to Him.

Even more millions accept that they came from Mars after all and returned there. Most, but not all, give credit to Yato Ishurti for their leaving; these point out that even if Ishurti's reasoning was right down the line and even though his proposition to the Martians was backed by that tremendous affirmative, the Martians could hardly have been expected to react instan-

And on one point everything the Martians, take

taneously; somewhere a council of them would have had to meet and weigh their decision, make up their minds whether we were by now sufficiently sincere and sufficiently chastened. And that the Martians stayed only two weeks after Ishurti's speech, which is certainly not too long a time for such a decision to have been reached.

At any rate, no standing armies have been built up again and no country is planning sending any rockets to Mars, just on the *chance* that Ishurti was right, or partly right.

But not everybody, by any means, believes that either God or Ishurti had anything to do with the departure of the Martians.

One entire African tribe, for instance, knows that it was Bugassi's juju that sent the *gnajamkata* back to the *kat*.

One janitor in Chicago knows perfectly well that he drove away the Martians with his anti-extraterrestrial subatomic supervibrator.

And of course those last two are, and were given as, only random examples of the hundreds of thousands of *other* scientists and mystics who, each in his own way, had been trying his best to accomplish the same thing. And each naturally thought that he had finally succeeded.

And of course Luke knows that they're *all* wrong. But that it doesn't matter what they think since they all exist only in his mind anyway. And since he is now a very successful writer of Westerns, with four best sellers under his belt in four years and with a beautiful Beverly Hills mansion, two Cadillacs, a loved and loving wife and a pair of two-year-old twin sons, Luke is being very careful indeed how he lets his imagination work. He is very satisfied with the universe as he imagines it right now, and takes no chances.

And on one point concerning the Martians, Luke

Devereaux agrees with everybody else, including Oberdorffer, Bugassi and the Scandinavian.

Nobody, but nobody, misses them or wants them back.

AUTHOR'S POSTSCRIPT

My publishers write me:

> Before sending the manuscript of MARTIANS, GO HOME to the printer, we would like to suggest that you supply the story with a postscript to tell us and your other readers the *truth* about those Martians.
>
> Since you wrote the book, you, if anyone, must know whether they were really from Mars or hell, or whether your character Luke Devereaux was right in believing that the Martians, along with everything else in the universe, existed only in his imagination.
>
> It is unfair to your readers not to tell them.

Many things are unfair, including and particularly that request of my publishers!

I had wanted to avoid being definitive here, for the

truth can be a frightening thing, and in this case it *is* a frightening thing if you believe it. But here it is:

Luke is right; the universe and all therein exists only in his imagination. He invented it, and the Martians.

But then again, *I invented Luke.* So where does that leave him *or* the Martians?

Or any of the rest of you?

FREDRIC BROWN
Tucson, Arizona, 1955

Niven • Pournelle • Flynn
FALLEN ANGELS

In 1995 Earth finally had its act together. There were two manned space stations orbiting, one from the former Soviet Union, one from the United States. Even better, the human race had finally agreed that something had to be done about the environment—and was doing it, one green law after another. By the year 2020 the Greenhouse Effect was just a bad memory, and the air was a clean green dream.

There was only one problem. All that pollution, all that CO_2—the Greenhouse Effect itself—was the only thing holding off the next, regularly scheduled ice age! With the carbon dioxide gone the glaciers came, and came down fast. In the mid-21st century, the icebergs had reached North Dakota and weren't slowing down.

But by then an alliance of the most extreme "deep ecology" Greens and the zaniest of religious fundamentalists had taken over in the winter-bound U.S.—and they weren't about to give up their power merely because they were destroying civilization. And they needed a scapegoat. So they decided that it was the "air thievery" of the folks they left stranded in the orbiting space stations that was causing the New Ice Age.

FALLEN ANGELS is the story of two spacemen. Shot down and stranded on a hostile Earth, they think there is no hope for them. But they're wrong. Help is on the way. Help from the one nationally organized pro-technology group left on Earth; the only ones who would dare fly in the face of their unforgiving authoritarian government; the only ones foolish enough to risk everything to help two strangers from space. Science fiction fandom. *Angels* down. *Fans to the rescue*!

72052-X • 400 pp. • $5.95